After the Circus

English translations of works by Patrick Modiano

From Yale University Press
After the Circus
Paris Nocturne
Pedigree
Suspended Sentences

Also available or forthcoming
The Black Notebook
Catherine Certitude
Dora Bruder
Honeymoon
In the Café of Lost Youth
Lacombe Lucien
Missing Person
Out of the Dark
So You Don't Get Lost in the Neighborhood
The Occupation Trilogy (The Night Watch,
   Ring Roads, and La Place de l'Etoile)
Villa Triste
Young Once

After the Circus

A novel by Patrick Modiano

Translated from the French
by Mark Polizzotti

Yale UNIVERSITY PRESS · NEW HAVEN AND LONDON

A MARGELLOS
WORLD REPUBLIC OF LETTERS BOOK

The Margellos World Republic of Letters is dedicated to making literary works from around the globe available in English through translation. It brings to the English-speaking world the work of leading poets, novelists, essayists, philosophers, and playwrights from Europe, Latin America, Africa, Asia, and the Middle East to stimulate international discourse and creative exchange.

Designed by Nancy Ovedovitz.
Set in MT Baskerville type by Tseng Information Systems, Inc.
Printed in the United States of America.

Library of Congress Control Number: 2015940845
ISBN 978-0-300-21589-2 (paper : alk. paper)

A catalogue record for this book is available from the British Library. This paper meets the requirements of ANSI/NISO z39.48-1992 (Permanence of Paper).

10 9 8 7 6 5 4 3 2 1

For my parents

After the Circus

I was eighteen, and the man whose face I don't recall was typing up my legal status, address, and supposed student enrollment as fast as I could state them. He asked how I spent my free time.

I paused for a few seconds.

"I go to movies and bookstores."

"You don't *just* go to movies and bookstores."

He cited the name of a café. No matter how often I repeated that I'd never set foot in the place, I could tell he didn't believe me. Finally, he contented himself with typing the following:

"I go to movies and bookstores. I have never been to the Café de la Tournelle, at number 61 on the quay of that name."

Then more questions about my activities and my parents. Yes, I took literature courses at the university. There was no danger in telling him that lie: I really had enrolled in the program, but only to prolong my draft deferment. As for my parents, they were both abroad and I had no idea when they'd return, if ever.

Then he mentioned the names of a man and a woman and asked if I knew them. I answered no. He told me to think very carefully. If I didn't tell the truth, there could be serious consequences. The threat was delivered in a calm, indifferent voice. No, really, I didn't know those two individuals. He typed my answer, then handed me the sheet, at the bottom of which was written: "Seen and agreed to." I didn't bother looking over my deposition and signed with a ballpoint pen that was lying on the desk.

Before leaving, I asked why I'd had to submit to that interrogation.

"Your name was in someone's address book."

But he didn't say who that someone was.

"We'll be in touch if we need you again."

He saw me to the door of his office. In the hallway, on the leather bench, sat a girl of about twenty-two.

"You're next," he said to the girl.

She stood up. We exchanged glances. Through the door that he'd left ajar, I saw her sit down in the same chair that I'd occupied a moment earlier.

I found myself back on the quay. It was around five in the afternoon. I walked toward the Pont Saint-Michel, thinking that I might wait for the girl to come out after her interrogation. But I couldn't just loiter about police headquarters. I decided to bide my time in the café on the corner of Boulevard du Palais, where it meets the quay. And what if she had gone in the opposite direction, toward the Pont-Neuf? The thought never occurred to me.

I was seated near the window, my eyes fixed on the Quai des Orfèvres. Her interrogation lasted much longer than mine. Night had already fallen when I saw her walking toward the café.

As she was passing by, I tapped on the window with the back of my hand. She looked at me in surprise, then came inside to join me.

She sat down at my table as if we knew each other and had made a date. She was the first to speak.

"Did they ask you a lot of questions?"

"My name was in someone's address book."

"Do you know who?"

"They wouldn't tell me. But maybe you can shed some light."

She knitted her brow.

"Shed light on what?"

"I figured your name must have been in that address book, too, and they were questioning you about the same thing."

"No. With me, it was just to give evidence."

She seemed preoccupied. It felt like she was slowly forgetting I was there. I kept silent. Then she smiled. She asked how old I was. I said twenty-one, making myself three years older: legal age, at the time.

"Do you have a job?"

"I deal in used books," I said randomly, in a tone I tried to make convincing.

She looked at my face, no doubt wondering if she could trust me.

"Will you do me a favor?" she asked.

*   *   *

At Place du Châtelet, she wanted to take the metro. It was rush hour. We stood squeezed together near the doors. At every station, the riders getting off pushed us onto the platform. Then we got back on with the new passengers. She leaned her head on my shoulder and said with a smile that "no one could find us in this crowd."

At the Gare du Nord metro stop, we were carried along in the flood of travelers heading for the commuter trains. We crossed through the train station lobby, and in the checkroom she opened a locker and pulled out a black leather suitcase.

I carried the suitcase, which was rather heavy. It occurred to me that it contained more than just clothes. The metro again, same line but in the opposite direction. This time we found seats. We got off at Cité.

At the end of the Pont-Neuf, we waited for the light to turn red. I was feeling increasingly anxious. I wondered how Grabley would greet us when we arrived at the apartment. Shouldn't

I tell her about Grabley, so that his presence there wouldn't catch her off guard?

We walked past the Hôtel des Monnaies. I heard the clock on the Institut de France chime nine P.M.

"Are you sure no one will mind if I come to your place?" she asked.

"Nope. No one."

There were no lights in the apartment windows facing the quay. Had Grabley gone to his room, on the courtyard side? Normally he parked his car in the middle of the little square that forms a recess between the Hôtel des Monnaies and the Institut, but it wasn't there.

I opened the door on the fourth floor and we walked through the foyer. We entered the room that had served as my father's office. Light fell from a naked bulb dangling from the ceiling. No furniture left, except for an old couch with dark red leaf patterns.

I set the suitcase down next to the couch. She went to the window.

"You have a nice view . . ."

To the left was one end of the Pont des Arts and the Louvre. Directly in front, the tip of Ile de la Cité and the small Vert-Galant park.

We sat on the couch. She looked around her and seemed amazed by the sparseness of the room.

"Are you moving out?"

I told her that, unfortunately, we had to vacate the premises in a month. My father had gone to Switzerland to live out his days.

"Why Switzerland?"

It really was too long a story for that evening. I shrugged. Grabley would be back any minute. How would he react when he saw the girl and her suitcase? I was afraid he would call my father in Switzerland, and that the latter, in a last gasp of parental dignity, would try to play the noble paterfamilias, lecture me about my studies and endangered future. But he was wasting his time.

"I'm tired . . ."

I suggested she lie down on the couch. She hadn't removed her raincoat. I remembered that the heating no longer worked.

"Are you hungry? I can go get something from the kitchen . . ."

She sat on the couch, legs folded under her, resting on her heels.

"Don't go to any trouble. Maybe just something to drink . . ."

The light in the foyer had gone off. The bow window in the wide front hall leading to the kitchen lit the room with pale glimmers, as if there were a full moon out. Grabley had left the light on in the kitchen. In front of the old dumbwaiter stood an ironing board on which I recognized the trousers of his glen plaid suit. He ironed his own shirts and other clothes. On the folding table, where I sometimes took my meals with him, was an empty yogurt jar, a banana peel, and a packet of instant coffee. He must have eaten in. I found two yogurts, a slice of salmon, some fruit, and a bottle of whiskey three-quarters empty. When I returned, she was reading one of the magazines that Grabley had let pile up for several weeks on the office mantelpiece, "risqué" periodicals, as he called them, for which he had a great fondness.

I set the tray down in front of us, on the floor.

She had left the magazine open next to her and I could make out the black-and-white photo of a naked woman, seen from behind, hair tied in a ponytail, left leg extended, right leg bent, her knee resting on a mattress.

"Interesting reading matter you've got . . ."

"No, those aren't mine . . . They belong to a friend of my father's."

She bit into an apple and poured herself some whiskey.

"What have you got in that suitcase?" I asked.

"Oh, nothing much . . . Some personal effects . . ."

"It was heavy. I thought it was stuffed with gold bricks."

She gave me a sheepish smile. She explained that she lived in a house not far from Paris, near Saint-Leu-la-Forêt, but the owners had come back unexpectedly last night. She preferred to leave, as she didn't really get along with them. Tomorrow she would go to a hotel, until she could find a permanent place to live.

"You can stay here as long as you like."

I was sure that Grabley, after his initial surprise, would have no objections. As for my father, what he thought no longer mattered.

"Are you getting sleepy?"

I intended to give her the upstairs bedroom. I would sleep on the office couch.

I led the way, suitcase in hand, up the small inner staircase to the fifth floor. The room was as sparsely furnished as the office. A bed shoved against the back wall. The nightstand and bedside lamp were gone. I switched on the fluorescent lights in the two display cases, on either side of the fireplace, where my father kept his collection of chess pieces, although these had disappeared, along with the small Chinese armoire and the fake Monticelli canvas that had left a discoloration on the sky-blue paneling. I had consigned those three objects to an antiques dealer, a certain Dell'Aversano, for him to sell.

"Is this your room?" she asked.

"Yes."

I had set the suitcase in front of the fireplace. She went to the window, like before, in the office.

"If you look all the way to the right," I told her, "you can see the statue of Henri IV and the Tour Saint-Jacques."

She gazed distractedly at the rows of books between the two windows. Then she lay down on the bed and removed her shoes with a casual flick of her foot. She asked where I was going to sleep.

"Downstairs on the couch."

"Stay here," she said. "I don't mind."

She had kept on her raincoat. I turned off the lights in the display cases. I lay down next to her.

"Doesn't it feel cold to you?"

She moved closer and gently rested her head on my shoulder. Lights and shadows shaped like window grates slid across the walls and ceiling.

"What's that?" she asked.

"The tour boat passing by."

I awoke with a start. The front door had slammed.

She was lying against me, nude inside her raincoat. It was seven in the morning. I heard Grabley's footsteps. He was making a phone call in the office. His voice grew louder and louder, as if he was arguing with someone. Then he left the office and went into his room.

She woke up as well and asked what time it was. She told me she had to be going. She had left some belongings in the house in Saint-Leu-la-Forêt and wanted to collect them as soon as possible.

I offered her breakfast. There was still some instant coffee in the kitchen and one of the boxes of Choco BN biscuits that Grabley always bought. When I returned to the fifth floor with the tray, she was in the large bathroom. She emerged, dressed in her black skirt and pullover sweater.

She said she would call me early that afternoon. She didn't have any paper on which to

jot down my number. I took a book from the
shelves and tore out the flyleaf, on which I wrote
my name, address, and phone number: DANTON
55-61. She folded the paper in four and shoved
it in one of her raincoat pockets. Then her lips
brushed mine and she said in a low voice that
she was grateful and was looking forward to seeing me again.

She walked along the quay toward the Pont
des Arts.

I stood at the window for a few minutes,
watching her distant silhouette cross the bridge.

I stashed the suitcase in the storage closet at
the top of the stairs. I laid it flat on the floor. It
was locked. I lay down again and breathed in
her scent from the hollow of one of the pillows.
She would eventually tell me why they'd questioned her yesterday afternoon. I tried to recall
the names of the two people the detective had
mentioned, asking whether I knew them. One
of them sounded something like "Beaufort" or

"Bousquet." In whose address book had they found my name? Was he just trying to get information about my father? He'd asked which foreign country my father had gone to. I had covered his tracks by answering Belgium.

The week before, I had accompanied my father to the Gare de Lyon. He was wearing his old navy blue overcoat and his only luggage was a leather bag. We were early, and we waited for the Geneva train in the large restaurant on the upper level, from which we overlooked the lobby and railway tracks. Was it the late afternoon light? The golden hue on the ceiling? The chandeliers that shone down on us? My father suddenly seemed old and tired, like someone who has been playing "cat and mouse" for far too long and is about to give up.

The only book he brought with him for the trip was called *The Hunt*. He had recommended it to me several times, because the author mentioned our apartment, where he'd lived twenty years earlier. What a strange coincidence . . .

Hadn't my father's life, in certain periods, re-
sembled a hunt in which he was the prey? But so
far, he'd managed to elude his captors.

We were facing each other over our coffee.
He was smoking, cigarette dangling from the
corner of his lips. He talked about my "schooling" and my future. As he saw it, it was all well
and good to want to write novels, as I intended,
but it was safer to earn a few "diplomas." I kept
quiet, listening to him. Words like "diplomas,"
"stable situation," "profession" sounded odd in
his mouth. He pronounced them with respect
and a kind of nostalgia. After a while, he fell
silent, exhaled a cloud of smoke, and shrugged.

We didn't exchange another word until
he climbed onto the train and leaned out the
lowered window. I had remained on the platform.

"Grabley will live with you in the apartment.
Afterward, we'll make a determination. You'll
have to rent someplace else."

But he had said it without any conviction.
The train for Geneva lurched forward, and at

that moment it felt as if I were seeing that face and that navy blue coat pull away forever.

At around nine o'clock, I went down to the fourth floor. I had heard Grabley's footsteps. He was sitting on the office couch in his plaid bathrobe. Next to him was a tray carrying a cup of tea and a Choco BN. He hadn't shaved and his features were drawn.

"Good morning, Obligado . . ."

He called me by that nickname because of a friendly wager we'd had. One evening, we had arranged to meet in front of a cinema on Avenue de la Grande-Armée. He had told me to get off at the Obligado metro stop. The stop was really called Argentine, but he refused to believe it. We had made a bet, which I'd won.

"I only got two hours' sleep last night. I made my 'rounds.'"

He stroked his blond mustache and squinted.

"Same places as usual?"

"The very ones."

His "rounds" invariably started at eight

o'clock at the Café des Deux Magots, where he had an aperitif. Then he crossed over to the Right Bank and stopped at Place Pigalle. He stayed in that neighborhood until dawn.

"And what about you, Obligado?"

"I put a girlfriend up last night."

"Does your father know?"

"No."

"You should ask him if it's all right. I'm sure I'll be getting a call."

He imitated my father when he wanted to appear serious and responsible, but it rang even less true than the original.

"And what sort of young lady is she?"

His face took on the unctuous expression with which he suggested, every Sunday morning, that I go to Mass with him.

"First of all, she's not a young lady."

"Is she pretty?"

I saw on his face the smug, flattering smile of the traveling salesman in some random station bar who over a beer tells you how he got lucky.

"*My* girlfriend last night wasn't too bad either . . ."

His tone became aggressive, as if we were suddenly in competition. I no longer remember what I felt at the time, with that seated man, in the empty office that looked as if it had been vacated at a moment's notice, its furniture and paintings pawned or repossessed. He was my father's stand-in, his factotum. They had met when very young on a beach on the Atlantic coast, and my father had corrupted this petty bourgeois Frenchman. For thirty years, Grabley had lived in his shadow. The only habit he retained from his childhood and good upbringing was to attend Mass every Sunday.

"Will you introduce me to your girlfriend?"

He gave me a complicit wink.

"We could even go out together, if you like . . . I'm fond of young couples."

I pictured us, her and me, in Grabley's car as it crossed over the Seine and headed toward Pigalle. A young couple. One evening I'd accompanied him to the Deux Magots, before he headed off on his usual "rounds." We were sitting near the windows. I had been surprised to see him greet in passing a couple of about twenty-five: the woman blonde and very graceful, the man dark and overly elegant. He had even gone to talk to them, standing next to their table, while I watched from my seat. Their age and appearance marked such a sharp contrast with Grabley's old-world manners that I wondered what fluke could have brought them together. The man seemed amused by what Grabley was saying, but the woman was more detached. Taking his leave, Grabley had shaken the man's hand and given the woman a ceremonious nod. When we left, he introduced them to me, but I've forgotten their names. Then he'd told me that the "young man" was a "very useful contact" and that he'd met him during his "rounds" in Pigalle.

"You seem pensive, Obligado . . . Are you in love?"

He had gotten up and was standing in front of me, hands in the pockets of his bathrobe.

"I need to spend all day at the office. I have to sift through the paperwork from seventy-three and move it out."

That was an office my father had rented on Boulevard Haussmann. I often used to go meet him there at the end of the afternoon. A corner room with a very high ceiling. Daylight entered through four French windows overlooking the boulevard and Rue de l'Arcade. Filing cabinets against the walls and a massive desk with an assortment of inkwells, blotters, and a writing case.

What did he do there? Each time, I would find him on the telephone. After thirty years, I happened across an envelope, on the back of which was printed the name of an ore refining company, the Société Civile d'Etudes et Traitements de Minerais, 73 Boulevard Haussmann, Paris 8.

"You and your girlfriend can come pick me up at seventy-three. We'll go have dinner together . . ."

"I don't think she's free this evening."

He seemed disappointed. He lit a cigarette.

"Well, anyway, call me at seventy-three to let me know your plans . . . I'd love to meet her . . ."

I was thinking I had to keep a bit of distance, or else we'd have him on our backs nonstop. But I've never been very good at saying no.

I remained in the office, reading and waiting for her call. She had said early afternoon. I'd set the phone beside me on the couch. When the clock hit three, I felt a vague disquiet that gradually worsened. I was afraid she'd never call. I tried to keep reading, in vain. Finally the telephone rang.

She still hadn't recovered the rest of her belongings in Saint-Leu-la-Forêt. We agreed to meet at six o'clock at the Tournon.

I had time to stop in at Dell'Aversano's to find out how much he intended to pay me for the fake Monticelli, little Chinese armoire, and chess pieces I'd left with him.

I crossed over the Pont-Neuf and followed the quays. Dell'Aversano had an antiques shop on Rue François-Miron, behind the Hôtel de Ville. I had met him two months earlier while selecting some used books from the shelves near the shop entrance.

He was a dark-haired man of about forty, with a Roman face and light-colored eyes. He spoke French with a slight accent. He had told me he imported antiques between France and Italy, but I didn't ask too many questions about that.

He was expecting me. He took me for coffee on the quay near the church of Saint-Gervais. He handed me an envelope, saying he'd buy the whole lot from me for seven thousand five hundred francs. I thanked him. I could live for a long time on that amount. Besides, I would soon have to leave the apartment and fend for myself.

As if he were reading my thoughts, Dell'Aversano asked what I planned to do with my life.

"You know, my offer still stands . . ."

He smiled at me. The last time I'd visited, he had said he could find me a job in Rome, with a bookseller he knew who needed a French assistant.

"Have you given it any thought? Could you see yourself living in Rome?"

I said yes. After all, I had no reason to remain in Paris. I was sure Rome would suit me fine. It would be a new life over there. I had to buy a map of the city, study it every day, learn the names of all the streets and squares.

"Do you know Rome well?" I asked him.

"Yes. I was born there."

I could drop in on him from time to time with my map and ask him about the various neighborhoods. That way, when I arrived in the city, I wouldn't feel disoriented.

Would she agree to come with me? I'd talk to her about it that evening. This might solve her problems as well.

"Did you live in Rome?"

"Of course," he said. "For twenty-five years."

"On what street?"

"I was born in the San Lorenzo district, and my last address was on Via Euclide."

I wanted to jot down the names of the district and the street, but I would try to remember them and look them up on the map.

"You can leave next month," he said. "My friend will find you a place to live. I don't think the work is very strenuous. You'll be dealing with French books."

He took a long drag on his cigarette, then, with a graceful gesture, as if in slow motion, he brought the coffee cup to his lips.

He told me that in Rome, when he was younger, he and his friends used to sit in a café and compete to see who could take the longest to drink an orangeade. It often lasted all afternoon.

I was early for our appointment, so I strolled along the alleys of the Jardin du Luxembourg. For the first time, it felt as if winter were approaching. Up until then, the autumn days had been sunny.

When I left the park, darkness was falling and the guards were preparing to lock the gates.

I chose a table at the back of the Tournon. The previous year, this café had been a refuge for me when I frequented the Lycée Henri-IV, the public library in the 6th arrondissement, and the Bonaparte cinema. I would often see a regular patron, the writer Chester Himes, always surrounded by jazz musicians and very pretty blonde women.

I had arrived at the Tournon at six o'clock, and by six-thirty she still wasn't there. Chester Himes was sitting on the bench next to the window, in the company of two women. One of them was wearing sunglasses. They were having a lively conversation in English. Customers drank their drinks, standing at the bar. To calm my nerves, I tried to follow the conversation between Himes and his friends, but they were talking too fast, except for the woman with a Scandinavian accent whom I could understand a little. She wanted to change hotels and was asking Himes the name of the place where he'd stayed when he'd first arrived in Paris.

I watched for her through the window. It was dark outside. A taxi halted in front of the Tournon. She got out. She was wearing her raincoat. The driver got out as well. He opened the trunk and handed her a suitcase, smaller than the one from last night.

She came toward me, suitcase in hand. She seemed glad to see me. She was just back from Saint-Leu-la-Forêt, where she'd been able to recover the rest of her effects. She had found a hotel room for the night. She asked me only to bring the suitcase back to my apartment. She preferred to leave it there, "in a safe place," with the other one. Again I told her these suitcases must be full of gold bricks. But she answered that they were merely objects of no particular value to anyone, except her.

I stated, trying to be persuasive, that she had been wrong to take a hotel room, since I could easily put her up at the apartment for as long as she liked.

"I'm better off at a hotel."

I sensed a certain reserve. She was hiding something from me, and I wondered whether it was because she didn't fully trust me or because she was afraid I'd be shocked if she told me the truth.

"And what about you, what have you been up to?"

"Nothing much. I sold some furniture from the apartment to get some money."

"Did it work out?"

"Yes."

"Did you need money?"

Her pale blue eyes stared at me.

"That's stupid. I could lend you some, if you like."

She smiled. The waiter came to take our order. She asked for a grenadine, and I followed suit.

"I've put some money aside," she said. "You can have it."

"That's very kind of you, but I think I've found a job."

I told her about Dell'Aversano's offer: to work in a bookstore in Rome. I hesitated a moment, then took the plunge:

"You could come with me . . ."

She didn't seem surprised by my suggestion.

"Yes . . . That might be a good idea. Do you know where you'd be living in Rome?"

"The bookseller I'll be working for is finding me a place."

She took a sip of grenadine. Its color went very well with the pale blue of her eyes.

"And when are you leaving?"

"In a month."

Silence fell between us. Like yesterday, in the café on Ile de la Cité, I had the impression she'd forgotten my presence and that she might just stand up and leave.

"I've always dreamed of going to live in London or Rome," she said.

Her gaze rested on me once more.

"You can feel safe in a foreign city . . . No one would know us . . ."

She had already made a similar remark in the metro yesterday evening. I asked if there was someone in Paris out to harm her.

"Not really. It's because of that interrogation yesterday . . . I feel like I'm being watched. They ask so many questions . . . They questioned me about people I used to know, but haven't seen in ages."

She shrugged.

"The problem is they didn't believe me. They must figure I still see those people . . ."

Some patrons sat down at the table next to ours. She leaned toward me.

"What about you? How many were there when you were questioned?"

"Just one. The one who was there when you went in . . ."

"I had two. The second one came in later. He pretended just to be dropping by, but he started in with his own questions. The other kept on as well. I felt like a ping-pong ball."

"But who are these people you used to know?"

"I never knew them very well. I just met them once or twice."

She could see her answer didn't satisfy me.

"It's like you, when they told you your name was in an address book. You didn't even know whose it was . . ."

"So now you feel like you're being watched?"

She knitted her brow and gave me a strange look, as if she'd had a flicker of suspicion. I could guess what she was thinking: she had first seen me coming out of a detective's office, and three hours later I was still in the neighborhood, sitting at that café table.

"Do you think I've been assigned to keep an eye on you?" I asked with a smile.

"No. You don't look like a cop. And you're too young."

She didn't take her eyes off me. Then her face relaxed and we both burst out laughing.

This suitcase wasn't as heavy as the first. Following Rue de Tournon and Rue de Seine, we returned to the river. No lights on in the windows of the apartment. It was about seven-thirty, and Grabley, in the office at 73 Boulevard Haussmann, must still have been organizing those "papers" whose existence I hadn't even suspected. I had always thought the premises were as empty as the inkwells on the desk and that my father occupied them like a waiting room. And so I'd been surprised, thirty years later, to discover a tangible trace of his presence on Boulevard Haussmann, in the form of that envelope with the name of the ore refining company. But it's true that a name on the back of an envelope doesn't prove much of anything: you can read it over and over, and you're still in the dark.

I wanted to show her where I had stashed the
first suitcase and we climbed the small stairway
to the fifth floor. The door of the storage closet
opened on the left, just before the bedroom. The
closet smelled faintly of leather and sandalwood.
I set the suitcase I'd been carrying next to the
other and turned off the light. The key to the
storage closet was in the lock. I gave it two turns
and held the key out to her.

"You keep it," she said.

We went down to the office. She wanted to
make a phone call. She dialed a number but
there was no answer.

She hung up, looking disappointed.

"I'm supposed to have dinner with someone
tonight. Would you mind coming along?"

"If you like." I had called her by the familiar
tu without realizing it.

She started to add something, but was visibly
embarrassed.

"Could I ask you a big favor? I'd rather you
didn't mention yesterday's interrogation. And
also say you're my brother."

I wasn't surprised by her request. I was prepared to do anything she asked.

"Do you actually have a brother?"

"No."

But that was unimportant. The "someone" we were meeting for dinner was not a long-time acquaintance, and it was plausible that she hadn't yet told him about this brother who lived not far from Paris. Let's say in Montmorency, right near Saint-Leu-la-Forêt.

The telephone rang. She jumped. I answered. Grabley. He was still at 73 Boulevard Haussmann and he had put a lot of "files" in order. He had just had my father "on the line" and the latter had instructed him to get rid of all those papers as quickly as possible. He was hesitating between two possible alternatives: either wait until the concierge at number 73 put the building's garbage out on the curb and then stuff the "files" into the cans, or else simply chuck them down a manhole he'd spotted on Rue de l'Arcade. But in either case, he was afraid of attracting attention.

"My poor Obligado, I feel like I have to dispose of a corpse . . ."

He asked for news of my "girlfriend." No, the three of us couldn't get together this evening. She was having dinner at her brother's, somewhere between Montmorency and Saint-Leu-la-Forêt.

The taxi dropped us off at the corner of Avenue des Champs-Elysées and Rue Washington. She insisted on paying the fare.

We walked up Rue Washington on the left-hand side, then entered the first café we came to. Patrons were clustered around the pinball machine near the window, and while one of them was playing, the others chattered noisily.

We crossed the room. In the back, it narrowed to the dimensions of a corridor, along which, as in the restaurant car of a train, was a row of tables and benches in reddish imitation leather. A brown-haired man of barely thirty stood up as we approached.

She made the introductions.

"Jacques . . . My brother, Lucien . . ."

With a wave of his hand, he invited us to take the bench, facing him.

"We could eat here, if you like . . ."

And without even waiting for a reply, he raised his arm toward the waiter, who came to take our order. He chose the daily special for us. She seemed not to care about what she would eat.

He stared at me curiously.

"I wasn't aware that you existed . . . I'm very glad to know you . . ."

He stared at her in turn, then turned back toward me.

"It's true . . . I can see the resemblance . . ."

But I sensed some doubt in his remark.

"Ansart couldn't make it. We'll see him after dinner."

"I don't know," she said. "I'm feeling a bit tired, and we have to go all the way back to Saint-Leu-la-Forêt."

"No problem. I can drive you back in my car."

He had a pleasant face and a gentle voice. And there was a certain elegance to his dark flannel suit.

"So, what do you do for a living, Lucien?"

"He's still a student," she said. "Literature."

"I was a student, too. But in medicine."

He said this with a note of sadness in his voice, as if it were a painful memory. We were served a plate of smoked salmon and other fish.

"The owner is Danish," he said to me. "Perhaps you don't like Scandinavian food?"

"No, no, I like it very much."

She burst out laughing. He turned toward her.

"What's so funny?"

He used the familiar *tu* with her. How long had he known her and under what circumstances had they met?

"Lucien is what's funny."

She jerked her head at me. What exactly was their relationship? And why was she passing me off as her brother?

"I would gladly have had you over to my place," he said. "But I had nothing in the kitchen."

Having eaten only a few bites, she pushed away her plate.

"Aren't you hungry?"

"No, not right now."

"You look like something's bothering you . . ."

He took her wrist with a tender gesture. She tried to free herself, but he held fast and she ended up giving in. He held her hand in his.

"Have you known each other long?" I asked.

"Hasn't Gisèle ever mentioned me?"

"My brother and I haven't seen much of each other lately," she said. "He's been away a lot."

He gave me a smile.

"Your sister was introduced to me about two weeks ago by a friend . . . Pierre Ansart . . . Do you know Pierre Ansart?"

"No," she said, "he hasn't met him."

She seemed tired all of a sudden, ready to leave the table. But he was still holding on to her hand.

"Don't you know what's going on in your sister's life?"

He had spoken this last sentence in a suspicious tone.

She opened her handbag and took out a pair of sunglasses. She put them on.

"Gisèle is very private," I said casually. "She doesn't confide much."

It felt odd to say her name for the first time. Since yesterday, she hadn't even told me what it was. I turned toward her. Behind her shades, she seemed detached, distant, as if she hadn't been following the conversation, which, in any event, didn't concern her.

He checked his wristwatch. It was ten-thirty.

"Will your brother be coming with us to Ansart's?"

"Yes, but we won't stay long," she said. "I have to go back with him tonight to Saint-Leu-la-Forêt."

"In that case, I'll drive you there, then come back to see Ansart."

"You don't seem happy . . ."

"Nonsense," he said curtly. "I'm perfectly happy."

Perhaps he didn't want to argue with her in front of me.

"There's no point in you having to go so far

out of your way," she said. "We can take a cab back to Saint-Leu."

We climbed into a navy blue car that was parked in the service lane of the Champs-Elysées. She sat in front.

"Do you have a driver's license?" he asked me.

"No. Not yet."

She turned back toward me. I could sense her pale blue gaze behind the dark shades. She smiled.

"It's funny . . . I can't imagine my brother behind the wheel . . ."

He started up and drove slowly down the Champs-Elysées. She was still turned toward me. With an almost imperceptible movement of her lips, she blew me a kiss. I leaned my face closer to hers. I was on the verge of kissing her. The man's presence didn't deter me at all. I had such a desire to feel her lips on mine, to caress her, that he no longer mattered.

"You should persuade your sister to use this car. It would save her having to take subways and taxis . . ."

His voice made me jump and brought me back to reality. She turned away.

"You can have the car whenever you like, Gisèle."

"Can I have it tonight to get home to Saint-Leu-la-Forêt?"

"Tonight? If you insist . . ."

"I'd like to have it tonight. I need to get used to driving it."

"As you wish."

We skirted the Bois de Boulogne. Porte de la Muette. Porte de Passy. I had lowered the window slightly and was breathing in a draft of fresh air, the smell of wet earth and leaves. I would have liked to go walking with her down the alleys of the Bois, along the lakes, around the Cascade or the Croix Catelan, where I often went by myself in the late afternoon, taking the metro to escape the center of Paris.

He turned onto Rue Raffet and parked at the corner of Rue du Docteur-Blanche. I would come to know this area better several years later, and more than once I passed by the apartment house where we saw Ansart that evening. It was number 14, Rue Raffet. But topographical details have a strange effect on me: instead of clarifying and sharpening images from the past, they give me a harrowing sensation of emptiness and severed relationships.

We crossed the courtyard of the apartment house. In back was a small, one-story outbuilding. He rang at the door. A stocky, dark-haired man of about forty appeared. He was wearing an open-throated shirt under a tan cardigan. He kissed Gisèle on the cheeks and gave Jacques a hug.

We were in a white room. A blonde girl, twenty-something, was sitting on a red couch. Ansart held out his hand with a wide smile.

"This is Gisèle's brother," Jacques said. "And this is Pierre Ansart."

"Pleased to know you," Ansart said to me.

He spoke in a deep voice, with a slight working-class accent. The blonde girl stood up and went to kiss Gisèle.

"This is Martine," Ansart said to me.

The blonde greeted me with a slight nod and a shy smile.

"So, you've been hiding this brother of yours from us?" said Ansart.

He gazed at the two of us, at her and me, with a sharp eye. Was he taken in by the ruse? All three of us sat in armchairs colored the same red as the couch. Ansart sat on the couch and put his arm around the blonde girl's shoulder.

"Did you have dinner on Rue Washington?"

Jacques nodded. A staircase spiraled up at the back of the room. Via the closed trap door, one could access what was probably the bedroom. To the left, the living room communicated with a large kitchen that must also have served as dining room, in which I noticed, from my chair, the whiteness of the gleaming new appliances.

Ansart caught me looking.

"It's a former garage that I converted into an apartment."

"It's very nice," I said.

"Would you like something to drink? Some herb tea?"

The blonde girl got up and walked to the kitchen.

"Four herb teas, Martine," Ansart said with paternalistic authority.

His eyes were still fixed on me, as if he were trying to gauge whom he was dealing with.

"You're very young . . ."

"I'm twenty-one."

I repeated my lie from the day before. She had removed her sunglasses and was staring at me as if seeing me for the first time.

"He's a student," Jacques said, looking at me as well.

I was embarrassed to be the focus of their attention. I started wondering what I was doing there, amid these people I didn't know. Even she—I didn't know her any better than the others.

"A student of what?" Ansart asked.

"Literature," said Jacques.

The blonde girl came out of the kitchen, carrying a tray that she set on the carpet among us. With graceful movements, she handed each of us a cup of tea.

"And when will you be finished with your studies?" Ansart asked me.

"In two or three years."

"Meantime, I suppose it's your parents who provide for you . . ."

His eyes were still fixed on me, as if I were some kind of curious specimen. I thought I discerned in Ansart's voice an amused contempt.

"You're lucky to have such good parents to help you out . . ."

He'd said it with a touch of bitterness and his gaze clouded over.

What could I reply? I briefly thought of my father and his escape to Switzerland, Grabley, the empty apartment, Dell'Aversano, my mother somewhere in southern Spain . . . All things considered, it was better to have him think of me as a nice young man being supported by his parents.

"You're wrong," she said suddenly. "Nobody's helping him out. My brother's making his own way . . ."

I was moved that she'd come to my rescue. I had forgotten we were brother and sister, and so naturally we had the same parents.

"Besides, we don't have any family left. It simplifies things . . ."

Ansart gave us a wide smile.

"My poor children . . ."

The atmosphere relaxed. The blonde girl poured some more tea into our empty cups. She seemed very fond of Gisèle and called her *tu*.

"Are you going by the restaurant this evening?" Jacques asked.

"Yes," said Ansart.

Gisèle turned to me.

"Pierre owns a small restaurant in the neighborhood."

"Oh, it's nothing much," Ansart said. "The place was on the skids and I took it over, no good reason, just for fun . . ."

"We'll take you for dinner there some evening," said Jacques.

"I don't know if my brother will come. He never goes out."

She had used a firm tone of voice, as if she wanted to protect me from them.

"But it would be so nice to go out, just the four of us," the blonde girl said.

She rested her candid gaze first on Gisèle, then on me. She seemed to wish us well.

"Lucien and I have to get back to Saint-Leu-la-Forêt," Gisèle said.

"Can't you stay just a little longer?" Jacques said.

I took a deep breath and said in a firm voice, "No, we really should be going. My sister and I have been having problems with the house . . ."

She had surely mentioned the house in Saint-Leu-la-Forêt. Perhaps she had told them details I didn't know about.

"So, are you taking the car?" Jacques asked.

"Yes."

He turned to Ansart.

"I'm lending her my car. You don't mind if I borrow one of yours, do you?"

"Sure. We'll go get one from the garage later on."

We stood up, she and I. She gave the blonde girl a kiss. I shook hands with Ansart and Jacques.

"When will I see you again?" Jacques asked her.

"I'll call you."

He seemed dismayed that she was leaving.

"Take good care of your sister."

He handed her the car keys.

"Careful on the road. If there's no answer at my place tomorrow, call me at the restaurant."

For his part, Ansart was looking me over carefully, as he'd done when we arrived.

"I'm very pleased to know you. If you ever need anything . . ."

I was surprised by his sudden solicitude.

"It can be hard, being your age. I know all too well—I've been there myself . . ."

His eyes wore a sad expression that clashed with his resonant voice and energetic bearing.

The blonde girl saw us to the door.

"We could get together tomorrow, if you like," she said to Gisèle. "I'll be home all day."

On the threshold, in the dim light of the courtyard, the girl's face looked even younger. It occurred to me that Ansart was old enough to be her father. We crossed the courtyard and she remained standing there, following us with her eyes. Her silhouette stood out against the lit doorway. She looked as if she wanted to come with us. She raised her arm in good-bye.

We had forgotten where the car was parked. We walked down the street, searching for it.

"What if we just take the metro?" she said. "That car is complicated to drive . . . and besides, I think I've lost the keys."

Her casual tone made me break out in hysterical laughter, which then seized her as well.

Soon we couldn't control ourselves. Our howls echoed down the silent, empty street. When we reached the end of it, we started back up in the opposite direction, on the other sidewalk. We finally found the car.

She opened the door, after trying out all four keys on the keychain. We settled into the leather seats.

"Now we just have to get it moving," she said.

She managed to start the engine. She made a sudden jerk backward, then braked just as the car had reversed onto the sidewalk and was about to ram into the door of a building.

She drove off in the direction of the Bois de Boulogne, bust rigid, face straining slightly forward, as if she'd never been behind a wheel before.

We reached the quays via Boulevard Murat. At the place where the street made a right angle, she said, "I used to live around here."

I should have asked when that was and under what circumstances, but I let the moment pass. When you're young, you neglect certain details that might become precious later. The boulevard made another sharp turn and headed toward the Seine.

"So, do you think I'm a good driver?"

"Very good."

"You're not afraid to be in the car with me?"

"Not at all."

She pressed on the accelerator. At Quai Louis-Blériot, the road narrowed, but she sped up even more. A red light. I was afraid she would run it. But no, she screeched to a halt.

"I think I'm getting the hang of this car."

Now she was driving at normal speed. We arrived at the gardens of Trocadéro. She crossed the river over the Pont d'Iéna, then skirted the Champ-de-Mars.

"Where are we going?" I asked.

"To my hotel. But first, I need to pick up something I forgot."

We were on the deserted square of the Ecole Militaire. The huge edifice seemed abandoned. We could make out the Champ-de-Mars, like a prairie gently sloping toward the Seine. She continued straight ahead. The dark mass and surrounding wall of a barracks. At the end of the street, I saw the viaduct of the elevated metro. We stopped in front of a building on Rue Desaix.

"Will you wait for me? I won't be long."

She had left the key on the dashboard. She disappeared into the building. I wondered whether she'd ever return. After a while, I got out of the car and planted myself in front of the entrance, a glass door with wrought iron. There might have been a rear exit. She would vanish, leaving me with this useless automobile. I tried to talk sense to myself. Even if she did give me the slip, I had several reference points: the café on Rue Washington where Jacques was a regular, Ansart's apartment, and especially the suitcases. Why was I so afraid she might disappear? I had met her only twenty-four hours ago and knew almost nothing about her. Even her name I'd learned through others. She couldn't keep still; she flitted from place to place as if running from some danger. I didn't think I could hold on to her.

I was pacing back and forth on the sidewalk. Behind me, I heard the entrance door open and close. She walked up quickly. She was no longer wearing her raincoat, which she had folded over her arm, but a full-length fur.

"Were you going to leave?" she asked. "Had you gotten tired of waiting?"

She gave me a worried smile.

"Not at all. I thought you'd skipped out on *me*."

She shrugged.

"That's ridiculous . . . Whatever made you think that?"

We walked to the car. I had taken her raincoat and was carrying it over my shoulder.

"That's a nice coat," I said.

She seemed embarrassed.

"Oh, yes . . . It's a lady I know . . . She lives here . . . a seamstress . . . I'd given her the coat so she could resew the hem."

"Did you tell her you'd be coming over so late?"

"It was no bother . . . She works at night . . ."

She was hiding the truth from me and I was tempted to ask more specific questions, but I held back. She would eventually get used to me. Little by little she'd learn to trust me and tell me everything.

We were back in the car. I laid her raincoat on the back seat. She pulled away from the curb, gently this time.

"My hotel is right near here . . ."

Why had she chosen a hotel in this neighborhood? It wasn't just chance. Something must have kept her around here, like an anchor point. Perhaps the presence of that mysterious seamstress?

We took one of the streets that led from Avenue de Suffren toward Grenelle, on the border of the 7th and 15th arrondissements. We stopped in front of a hotel, its façade bathing in the glow from the lit sign of a garage at a bend in the road. She rang at the door, and the night porter came to open for us. We followed him to the reception desk. She asked for the key to her room. He shot me a suspicious glance.

"Can you fill out a registration? I'll need to see some ID."

I didn't have my papers on me. In any case, I was still a minor.

He had put the key on the reception desk. She picked it up nervously.

"This is my brother . . ."

The other hesitated for a moment.

"Well, you'll have to show me some proof. I need to see his papers."

"I forgot to bring them," I said.

"In that case, I can't let you go up with the young lady."

"Why not? He's my brother . . ."

Staring at the two of us in silence, he reminded me of the detective from the day before. The light accentuated his square jaw and balding head. A telephone sat on the counter. At any moment, I was expecting him to pick up the receiver and alert the nearest police station to our presence.

We made an odd couple and we must have looked rather suspicious, she and I. I remember the man's strong jaw, his lipless mouth, the calm contempt with which he stared at us. We were at his mercy. We were nothing.

I turned toward her:

"I must have left my ID when we had dinner with mom," I said in a timid voice. "Maybe mom has found it."

I stressed the word *mom* to give him a more reassuring impression of us. She, on the other hand, seemed quite prepared to have it out with the night porter.

She was holding the key. I plucked it from her hand and set it down gently on the desk.

"Come on . . . We'll go try to find that ID . . ."

I dragged her out by the arm. It was about

thirty feet to the hotel exit. I was sure the man was watching us. Walk as naturally as possible. Especially don't make it look like we're running away. And what if he locked the door, and we were caught in a trap? But no.

Once outside, I felt relieved. That night porter was no longer a threat.

"Would you like to go back to the hotel alone?"

"No. But I'm sure that if we'd insisted, he would have given in."

"I'm not."

"Were you scared of him?"

She looked at me with a mocking smile. I wished I could have confessed to her that I'd lied about my age, that I was only eighteen.

"So, where to now?" she asked.

"My place. We'll be much better off there than at the hotel."

In the car, as we followed Avenue de Suffren toward the quays, I felt the same apprehension as with the night porter. I wondered whether this car and that fur coat she was wearing wouldn't draw even more attention to us. I was afraid that at the next intersection, we might be stopped by one of those police roadblocks that were common in Paris at the time, when they checked for unaccompanied minors after midnight.

"Do you have your driver's license?"

"It must be in my handbag," she said. "Have a look."

Her handbag was sitting on the dashboard. There wasn't much in it and I immediately located the license. I was tempted to read it, so that I would finally know her name, address, and date and place of birth. But, out of discretion, I didn't.

"What about the registration—do we have that?"

"Probably . . . check in the glove compartment."

She shrugged. She seemed not to care about all the dangers I dreaded for us. She had switched on the radio, and gradually the music calmed me down. I felt confident again. We hadn't done anything wrong. What could anyone hold against us?

"We should head to the South with this car," I said to her.

"I thought you wanted to go to Rome."

Up until then, I had imagined traveling to Rome by train. Now I tried to imagine us driving along the highway. First we would go to the South of France. Then we'd cross the border at Ventimiglia. With just a little luck, everything would go smoothly. Since I was underage, I'd draft a letter supposedly signed by my father, authorizing a trip abroad. I was an old hand at this type of forgery.

"Do you think they'd lend us the car?"

"Sure . . . Why wouldn't they?"

She didn't want to give me a straight answer.

"Well, you haven't known them very long . . ."

She remained silent. I returned to the attack.

"That fellow, Jacques—did you meet him through Ansart?"

"Yes."

"And what does Jacques do for a living?"

"He and Ansart are in business together."

"So how did you meet Ansart?"

"In a café."

She added:

"Jacques lives in a very nice apartment on Rue Washington. His full name is Jacques de Bavière . . ."

After that, I often heard that name on her lips: Jacques de Bavière. Did I mishear? Wasn't it a more prosaic name, like de Bavier or Debaviaire? Or simply a pseudonym?

"He's a Belgian national, but he's been living in France forever. He lives with his stepmother on Rue Washington."

"His *stepmother*?"

"Yes, his father's widow."

We had arrived at the Pont de la Concorde. Instead of turning onto Boulevard Saint-Germain, she crossed the Seine.

"I prefer taking the quays," she said.

"This Jacques de Bavière . . . He seems to be in love with you . . ."

"Perhaps. But I don't want to live with him. I want to retain my independence."

"You prefer living in Saint-Leu-la-Forêt?"

I had adopted a sarcastic tone, as if I didn't believe in the existence of that house in Saint-Leu-la-Forêt.

"I have a right to my own life . . ."

"Someday you'll have to take me to Saint-Leu . . ."

She smiled.

"Are you making fun of me?"

"Not in the slightest. I'd be very curious to see your house . . ."

"Unfortunately I stopped living there yesterday—as you know very well . . ."

The Pont-Neuf. We followed the same route that we'd taken on foot the evening before. She parked the car in the recess on Quai de Conti, at the corner of the cul-de-sac.

The windows of both the office and the adjacent bedroom were lit. This time, we wouldn't be able to avoid Grabley, and the prospect made me nervous. I said:

"We'll go in on tiptoe."

But just as we were crossing the foyer in the semidarkness, Grabley opened the door to the bedroom.

"Who's there? Is that you, Obligado?"

He was wearing his plaid bathrobe.

"You could at least introduce me . . ."

"Gisèle," I said in an unsure voice.

"Henri Grabley."

He had moved toward her and held out a hand that she didn't shake.

"Delighted to meet you. Please forgive me for greeting you in this attire."

He was playing master of the household. Moreover, his entire person corresponded so perfectly to that empty apartment . . .

"Mister Grabley is a friend of my father's," I said.

"His oldest friend."

With a gesture, he bade us enter the room, adjacent to the office, that had never had a very determinate function: sometimes it was a living room—the furniture used to consist of a midnight-blue sofa, two wing chairs of the same color, and a coffee table—sometimes a "guest room."

The curtainless windows looked out on the quay.

"I was getting fed up with my view of the courtyard, so I moved in here. Do I have your permission, Obligado?"

"Make yourself at home."

He had walked into the room, but she and I remained on the threshold. A mattress was lying on the floor, in the left-hand corner. Light came from a naked bulb in a lamp base. There wasn't any furniture left. On the marble mantelpiece were a large radio and the black oilskin bags Grabley sometimes used for his morning shopping.

"Shall we go into the office instead?"

He kept his eyes fixed on her, a fatuous smile on his face, his head slightly raised.

"You're very lovely, Miss . . ."

She didn't react, but I was afraid she would leave because of him.

"I hope you won't hold my frankness against me, Miss."

Our silence was making him feel awkward. He turned to me.

"I haven't been able to reach your father. The phone number he gave me doesn't answer."

No surprise there. I could even foresee that number ringing in the void for all eternity.

"Just keep trying," I told him. "He'll answer eventually."

He looked hapless, standing there before us like an old ham who can't win over the audience.

"Hey, what if the three of us had dinner tomorrow?"

"I don't know if Gisèle is free."

I looked to her for support.

"That's very kind of you, sir, but I'm afraid I won't be able to come in to the city tomorrow evening."

I was grateful to her for adopting that courteous tone—I'd been afraid she would answer much more cuttingly. I suddenly felt sorry for

Grabley, with his blond mustache and shopping bags on the mantelpiece; for my father, who had hightailed it . . . Today, I again see that scene, from a distance. Behind the panes of a window, in muted light, I can make out a blond man in his fifties wearing a plaid bathrobe, a girl in a fur coat, and a young man . . . The light bulb in the lamp base is too small and too weak. If I could go back in time and return to that room, I would change the bulb. But in brighter light, the whole thing might well dissolve.

In the fifth-floor bedroom, she was lying against me. I could hear muted music and an announcer's droning voice.

Grabley was listening to the radio downstairs.

"There's something weird about that guy," she said. "What does he do?"

"Oh, he's a bit of a jack of all trades."

One day, I had come across a wallet he'd left in the office. Among the other documents it contained, one very old one in particular had raised my eyebrows: an application to be listed in the

Business Register as a greengrocer in the pro-
duce market in Reims.

"And what about your father? Is he like that
too?"

For the first time, she had used the familiar *tu*.

"No, not exactly . . ."

"Did he go to Switzerland because he was in
trouble here in France?"

"Yes."

None of this seemed to bother her much.

"What about you? Do you have any family?"
I asked her.

"Not really."

She looked me in the eye and smiled.

"I have a brother named Lucien . . ."

"But what do you do for a living?"

"A little of everything . . ."

She knitted her brow, as if searching for the
right words. She finally said:

"I was even married once."

I pretended not to have heard. The slightest
word or movement might interrupt this confi-

dence. But she fell silent again, eyes fixed on the ceiling.

Reflections skidded across the walls. Their shape and movement were like foliage rustling and trembling in the wind. It was the last tour boat passing by, its searchlights aimed at the building façades along the quays.

The next day was Saturday. The sunshine and blue sky contrasted with the gray and cloud cover of the day before. One of the booksellers on the quay had already opened his stall. I experienced a holiday atmosphere that I'd already felt on the rare Saturdays in my past when I awoke in this same room, surprised to find myself far away from the boarding school dormitory.

That morning, she seemed more relaxed than the previous day. I thought of our upcoming departure for Rome and decided to buy myself a map of the city as soon as possible. Then I asked if she'd like to take a walk in the Bois de Boulogne.

Grabley had left a note in the office:

Dear Obligado,

I have to go back to Boulevard Hausmann to get rid of the rest of the papers your father left behind. This evening I make my "rounds." If you and your friend would like to join me, let's meet at

eight o'clock at the Magots. That girl is really quite
charming . . . Try to bring her along . . . I would be
delighted to introduce you this evening to someone
who isn't too bad herself.
H. G.

She went to make sure the suitcases were still
in the storage closet. Then she told me she had
to go get something before noon somewhere
near the Quai de Passy. That worked out well,
as it was on the way to the Bois de Boulogne.

As we were getting into the car, I asked her
to wait for me a moment and I ran to the bookseller's stall. In a row of books about travel and
geography, I found an old guide to Rome, and
this coincidence struck me as auspicious.

We were now used to this car, and I even felt
as if it had always belonged to us. There was
very little traffic that Saturday morning, as during those vacation weeks when most Parisians
have left the city. We crossed over to the Right
Bank via the Pont de la Concorde. The quays
were even emptier on that side. After the gar-

dens of Trocadéro, we stopped at the corner of Rue de l'Alboni, beneath the elevated metro.

She said she had to go on alone. She would meet me in an hour at the café on the quay.

She turned around and waved good-bye.

I wondered if she was going to vanish for good. The evening before, I'd had a reference point: I had seen her enter a building. But now, she didn't even want me to accompany her all the way. I was never sure of anything with her.

I preferred to walk rather than just sit and wait in that café, and one by one I took the neighboring streets and the stairways with their balusters and streetlamps. Later, I would often return to that area, and each time the stairways on Rue de l'Alboni reminded me of the Saturday when I had walked around there, waiting for her. It was November, but in my memory, because of the sun that day, a summer light bathes the neighborhood. Dappled sunlight on the sidewalks and shadows beneath the metro viaduct. A dark, narrow passageway that was once a rustic path rises through the buildings up to Rue Raynouard. At night, at the exit of the Passy metro stop, the streetlamps cast a pale light on the foliage.

The other day, I wanted to reconnoiter the area one last time. I emerged into that zone of administrative pavilions on the banks of the Seine. They were demolishing most of them. Heaps of rubble and dilapidated walls, as if after a bombardment. The bulldozers cleared away the debris with sluggish movements. I headed back via Rue Charles-Dickens. I wondered what the address could have been, where she'd gone that Saturday. It was surely on Rue Charles-Dickens. When we had parted, I'd seen her turn left and, an hour later, I started heading to the café on the quay where we were to meet. I was walking along Rue Frémiet toward the Seine when I heard someone call my name. I turned around: she was coming toward me, holding a black Labrador on a leash.

The dog, when it saw me, started wagging its tail. It rested its two front paws on my legs. I petted it.

"That's funny . . . It's like he knows you."

"Is this your dog?" I asked.

"Yes, but I left him with someone for a while because I couldn't take care of him."

"What's his name?"

"Raymond."

She seemed delighted to have the dog back.

"So now, is there anything else you have to go get?"

"No, not for the moment."

She gave me a smile. She had probably noticed I was gently teasing her. The suitcases, the fur coat, the dog . . . Today I understand better those constant displacements to try to gather up the scattered pieces of a life.

The dog jumped into the car and lay down on the back seat as if this were his usual spot. She said that before we went to the Bois de Boulogne, she had to stop by Ansart's. She wanted to ask Jacques de Bavière if we could keep the car. Ansart and Jacques de Bavière always saw each other on Saturday, at the apartment or at Ansart's restaurant. So these people had their habits, and now I had more or less become one of them, without really knowing why. I was the traveler who boards a departing train and finds himself in the company of four strangers. And he wonders whether he hasn't got on the wrong train. But no matter . . . In his compartment, the others start making conversation with him.

I turned around toward the dog.

"And does Raymond know Ansart and Jacques de Bavière?"

"Oh, yes, he knows them."

She burst out laughing. The dog raised his head and looked at me, perking up his ears.

She'd had the dog when she met them for the first time. She still lived in Saint-Leu-la-Forêt then. The people to whom she'd entrusted the dog, after that, had a house near Saint-Leu and an apartment in Paris. They had brought the dog back to Paris for her today.

I wondered if I should believe her. These explanations sounded at once too extensive and incomplete, as if she were trying to bury the truth under a wealth of detail. Why had she stayed there for an hour if it was just to pick up her dog? And why hadn't she let me come with her? Who were these people?

I sensed it wasn't worth asking. I had only known her for forty-eight hours. It would just take a few days of intimacy for the barriers between us to crumble. Pretty soon, I'd know everything.

We stopped in front of the building on Rue Raffet and crossed the courtyard. She hadn't put the leash on the dog, but he followed us obediently. It was Martine, the blonde girl, who opened the door for us. She kissed Gisèle on the cheeks. Then she kissed me, too. I was startled by the familiarity.

Ansart and Jacques de Bavière were both sitting on the couch, looking at photographic enlargements, some of which were scattered on the rug at their feet. They didn't seem surprised to see us. The dog hopped onto the couch and was all over them.

"So, are you happy to get your dog back?" said Jacques de Bavière.

"Very."

Ansart shuffled together the photos and set them on the coffee table.

"Any problems with the car?" asked Jacques de Bavière.

"Not a one."

"Have a seat for two minutes. Take a load off," Ansart said with his slightly blue-collar accent.

We sat in the armchairs. The dog went to lie down at Gisèle's feet. Martine sat on the floor, between Jacques de Bavière and Ansart, her back resting against the front of the couch.

"I was wondering if we could hold on to the car a while longer," said Gisèle.

Jacques de Bavière smiled sarcastically.

"Of course. Keep it as long as you like."

"On just one condition . . ." said Ansart.

He raised his finger to ask for our attention. With his face split by a smile, it was as if he was going to tell a good joke.

"On condition that you do me a favor . . ."

He took a cigarette from the pack on the coffee table, then lit it nervously with a lighter. He looked me straight in the eye, as if I was the one he was addressing and Gisèle was already more or less in the know.

"So . . . It's very simple . . . You just have to deliver a message for me . . ."

Jacques de Bavière and Martine stared at the dog, which remained in its sphinxlike position at Gisèle's feet, but I had the feeling it was mainly to keep from looking awkward and not meet my gaze. Perhaps they were afraid I'd be shocked by Ansart's offer.

"It's nothing very complicated . . . Tomorrow afternoon, you'll go into a café—I'll tell you the one . . . You'll wait for this fellow to come in . . ."

He picked up one of the photos on the coffee table and showed it to us from where he sat. The face of a dark-haired man in his forties. Gisèle didn't seem very surprised by this proposal, but Ansart had surely noticed my distrust. He leaned toward me:

"Don't worry. It's the most ordinary thing in the world . . . This man is a business relation of mine . . . When he's settled at his table, one of you will go up to him and just say: 'Pierre Ansart is waiting for you in the car on the corner . . .'"

He smiled again, with a large, childlike smile. His face certainly radiated candor.

I would have liked to know what Gisèle thought of all this. She had leaned forward and picked up the print that Ansart had laid back on the coffee table. We both studied it. It looked like a blow-up of an ID photo. A face with regular features. Dark hair brushed back. Bare forehead.

Martine and Jacques de Bavière also looked at the other photos, which showed the same man from various angles, alone or with others.

"So what does he do?" I asked in a shy voice.

"A highly honorable profession," Ansart said, without elaborating. "So, you wait for this man to show up and you give him my message. This will take place in Neuilly, right near the Bois de Boulogne."

"And what happens afterward?" Gisèle asked.

"Afterward, you're free to do as you like. And

since I'm not in the habit of asking people to work for nothing, I can offer you two thousand francs apiece for handling this chore."

"Thanks very much, but I don't need any money," I said.

"Don't be silly, my boy. One always needs money at your age . . ."

The man's paternal tone, and the expression in his eyes, so gentle and so sad, suddenly made me feel warmly toward him.

There was bright sunshine all afternoon, but we were in that time of year when night falls at around five o'clock. Ansart proposed that we all go have lunch in his restaurant. It was located a bit farther north in the 16th arrondissement, on Rue des Belles-Feuilles. Ansart, Jacques de Bavière, and Martine got into a black automobile, and we followed them down the empty Saturday streets.

"Do you think we should do his favor for him?" I asked Gisèle.

"It doesn't commit us to anything . . ."

"But aside from this restaurant, you don't really know what he does for a living, do you?"

"No."

"It would be useful to know . . ."

"You think so?"

She shrugged. We caught up with them at a red light on Boulevard Suchet. The two cars waited side by side. Martine was sitting in back and smiled at us. Ansart and Jacques de Bavière were absorbed in a serious conversation. With a tap of his index finger, Jacques de Bavière flicked the ash from his cigarette through the half-open window.

"Have you ever been to his restaurant?"

"Yes, two or three times. You know, I haven't known them all that long myself . . ."

In fact, she had known them for only three weeks. There was nothing binding us to them, unless she was hiding something from me. I asked if she intended to keep seeing them. She explained that Jacques de Bavière had been very nice to her and had done her a huge favor the first time they'd met. He had even lent her some money.

"They're not the reason the police called you in the other day, are they?"

The idea had suddenly occurred to me.

"No, no, of course not . . ."

She knitted her brow and shot me a wary look.

"Listen, they absolutely can't find out that I was questioned . . ."

She had already urged the same thing the night before, without adding any details.

"Why? Will they get in trouble because of it?"

She had pressed on the gas pedal. The dog sat up on the back seat and leaned his head in the crook of my shoulder.

"They called me in because they found my name on a hotel register. But in any event, I would have gone to see them on my own . . ."

"How come?"

We had passed Ansart and Jacques de Bavière's car. We were driving very fast, and it seemed to me we had run a red light. I could feel the dog's breath on my neck.

"I left my husband and he's looking for me. The last months I was with him, he was constantly threatening me . . . I told the whole story to the police."

"Were you living with him in Saint-Leu-la-Forêt?"

"No."

She had answered curtly. She was already regretting having taken me into her confidence. I ventured another question:

"What kind of man is your husband?"

"Oh . . . Average . . ."

I realized I'd get nothing more out of her for now. The others had caught up with us. Jacques de Bavière leaned out of the open window and shouted:

"You think you're racing at Le Mans?"

And they sped past us, then slowed down. She did too. We were now driving behind them, so close that our bumpers were nearly touching.

"After lunch, can we go for a walk in the Bois de Boulogne?" I asked.

"Of course. We're not obliged to stay with them . . ."

I was happy to hear her say it. I felt dependent on adults and their whims. The boarding school existence I'd known for six years and the threat of an impending departure for the army made me feel as if I were stealing every instant of freedom and leading a sham life.

"That's true . . . It's not like we owe them anything . . ."

My remark made her laugh. The dog was still breathing on my neck, and now and again he ran his coarse tongue over my ear.

The restaurant had the same name as the street: the Belles Feuilles.

A small dining room. Pale wood trim. A mahogany bar. Tables covered with white tablecloths and red imitation-leather seats.

When we entered, three patrons were having lunch. We were greeted by the waiter, a brown-haired man of about thirty-five in a white jacket whom they called Rémy. He gave us a table in back. Gisèle hadn't removed her fur coat.

She said to Ansart:

"Do you think they could give the dog something to eat?"

"Of course."

He called Rémy over and we each ordered the daily special. Ansart stood up and walked over to the table with the patrons. He spoke to them very courteously. Then he came back to join us.

"So, what do you think of my establishment?" he asked me, favoring me with his wide smile.

"I like it a lot."

"It's an old working-class café I used to hang out in when I was your age, during the war. At the time, I never would have imagined I could turn it into a restaurant."

He was practically confiding in me. Because of my shyness? My attentive eyes? My age, which made him reminisce?

"From now on, you eat here on the house."

"Thank you."

Jacques de Bavière had gone to make a phone call at the bar. He was standing behind it, as if he owned the place.

"I have a very respectable clientele," Ansart said. "People from the neighborhood . . ."

"And are you involved with the restaurant, too?" I asked Martine.

"She just helped me out a bit with the decoration."

He rested an affectionate hand on her shoulder. I would have liked to know under what circumstances they had met, and also how Ansart and Jacques de Bavière had become acquainted. Ansart was a good ten years older. I pictured him at my age, one November evening, entering this café that probably wasn't called the Belles Feuilles back then. What was he doing around here at the time?

After lunch, we stood awhile chatting on the sidewalk. Gisèle said we had to go walk the dog in the Bois. Ansart offered to drop Jacques de Bavière off at his place on Rue Washington. We told them there was no need, and that Jacques de Bavière could have his car back. But no, he insisted we hold on to it. It was very kind of him.

I asked Ansart where in Neuilly we were supposed to carry out our curious mission the next evening.

It was on Rue de la Ferme, at the edge of the Bois.

"Are you thinking of checking the place out? Good idea. It's safer that way. Better to scope out all the exits in advance."

And he clapped me on the shoulder, his face split by his candid smile.

After Porte Dauphine, we followed the road

leading to the lakes and parked in front of the
Pavillon Royal. A sunny Saturday afternoon in
late autumn, like those Saturdays in my childhood when I used to arrive at that same spot
at the same time of day, on the number 63 bus
that stopped at Porte de la Muette. There was
already a line of people at the boat rental con-
cession.

We walked along the lake. She had let go
the dog's leash and he ran ahead of us in the
alley. When he had gone too far ahead, she
called him—"Raymond!"—and immediately
he turned back. We passed by the landing dock
where one could take a motorboat to the Chalet
des Iles.

"Do we have to see them again later?"

She raised her face and looked at me with her
pale blue eyes.

"It would be best," she said. "They can help
us . . . And besides, they lent us the car."

"Do you really think we have to do what they
asked?"

"Are you afraid?"

She had taken my arm and we followed the alley, which grew narrower and narrower, between the rows of trees.

"If we do favors for Pierre, we can ask him for anything we want. You know, Pierre's really very nice . . ."

"Like what?"

"Like helping us with this trip to Rome."

She hadn't forgotten the plan I'd mentioned. I had the guide to Rome in one of my pockets and had already looked at it several times.

"I'd be happier in Rome myself," she said.

I wanted her to explain her situation to me once and for all.

"But what *is* the story with your husband?"

She stopped walking. The dog had climbed up the embankment and was sniffing around the tree trunks. She gave my arm a tight squeeze.

"He's trying to find me, but he hasn't managed to so far. But even so, I'm always afraid I'll run into him."

"Is he in Paris?"

"Sometimes."

"Do Ansart and Jacques de Bavière know about all this?"

"No. But you have to be nice to them. They can protect me from him."

"And what does he do?"

"Oh . . . It depends on the day . . ."

We were at the Carrefour des Cascades. We strolled along the other side of the lake. She didn't confide much else, other than that she had got married at nineteen and that her husband was older. I suggested we take the car past where Ansart had set our mission.

We cut across the Bois to the edge of Neuilly and reached Rue de la Ferme. The meeting place was a bar and restaurant at the corner of Rue de Longchamp. The last rays of sunlight lingered on the sidewalks.

It felt odd to be back here. I knew this area well. I had often come here with my father and a friend of his, then with Charell and Karvé, two schoolmates. There wasn't a soul on Rue de la Ferme and the riding stables looked closed.

* * *

Night had already fallen when we returned to Ansart's. He and Jacques de Bavière were sitting on the red couch, like the first time. Martine carried a tray in from the kitchen, containing tea and petits fours.

The photos were still on the coffee table. I picked one up at random, but it was the one I had already seen.

"Do you think we'll be able to recognize him?" I asked Ansart.

"Oh, sure. There shouldn't be very many people in the café tomorrow evening . . . And I'll tell you a detail that will make him stand out immediately: the guy will surely be wearing riding breeches."

I took a deep breath to buck up my courage, then said:

"But why don't you go into the café yourself?"

Ansart gave me a sad, tender look that clashed with his wide smile.

"Here's the problem: I don't really have an appointment with this fellow tomorrow . . . It's a surprise . . ."

"A good surprise?"

He didn't answer. I think that if there hadn't been such tenderness in his eyes, I might have become concerned. Martine poured us some tea. Ansart dropped into each of our cups, Gisèle's and mine, a sugar cube that he held between his thumb and index finger.

"Not to worry," Jacques de Bavière said, looking distractedly at one of the photos. "We're just playing a little joke on him . . ."

I wasn't really convinced, but Gisèle, sitting next to me, seemed to find all this entirely natural. She drank her tea in little sips. She gave the dog a sugar cube.

"Does the man ride horses?" I asked to break the silence.

Jacques de Bavière nodded.

"I met him in a stable on Rue de la Ferme where I rent a stall for my horse."

Gisèle turned to me and, as if she wanted to steer the conversation onto more anodyne territory, said:

"Jacques has a lovely horse. He's called Deer Field."

"I don't know if I'll keep him much longer," said Jacques de Bavière. "Horses are expensive, and I don't really have the time to enjoy him."

He didn't have Ansart's faint working-class accent, and the existence of this horse piqued my curiosity. I would have liked to see his apartment on Rue Washington and that "stepmother" Gisèle had told me about.

"Tomorrow, you can come here first or go directly to Rue de la Ferme," said Ansart. "Don't forget, the appointment is at six o'clock sharp . . . Here, this is for you and your sister . . ."

And he handed me two envelopes that I didn't dare refuse.

We stopped near the end of the Champs-Elysées and had trouble finding a parking space. Outside, the air was as warm as a Saturday evening in spring.

We decided to go to the movies, but we didn't

want to leave the dog in the car. I figured that at the Napoléon, near Avenue de la Grande-Armée, they'd be more lenient about dogs than in the large first-run houses. And in fact, the cashier and the usherette let him come in with us. They were showing *The Wonderful Country.*

When we left the cinema, I suggested dinner in a restaurant. I still had on me the seven thousand five hundred francs from Dell'Aversano, to which I now added the two envelopes that Ansart had given me, each of which contained two thousand francs.

I wanted to invite her, but I was intimidated by the restaurants along the Champs-Elysées. I asked her to choose.

"We could go back to Rue Washington," she said.

I was afraid of running into Jacques de Bavière. She reassured me. He would be with Ansart and wouldn't be home until very late.

On Rue Washington, we sat near the street window.

"Jacques lives just across the way."

She pointed out the entrance to number 22.

I would rather have forgotten all about them, but it was difficult as long as we hadn't left Paris. Since she said those people could help us, I wanted to believe it. I just would have liked to know more about them.

"Have you been to Jacques de Bavière's apartment?" I asked.

"Yes, several times."

"I'd be curious to know what it's like where he lives . . ."

"His stepmother must be there."

After dinner, we crossed the street and, at the entrance to number 22, I had a moment's hesitation.

"No, forget it . . ."

But she insisted. We would tell the stepmother we had an appointment with Jacques de Bavière, or simply that we were in the neighborhood and thought we'd drop by.

"But isn't it kind of late to be paying a visit? Do you know this woman?"

"A little bit."

We went into number 22 and Gisèle rang at a door on the ground floor. Above the bell was a small silver plaque with a name engraved on it: Ellen James.

A woman's voice asked:

"Who is it?"

The door was equipped with a peephole. She must have been watching us.

"We're friends of Jacques," Gisèle said.

The door opened onto a blonde woman of about forty-five, wearing a black silk dress. A string of pearls around her neck.

"Ah, it's you . . ." she said to Gisèle. "I didn't recognize you."

She threw me a questioning look.

"My brother," Gisèle said.

"Come in . . ."

Frosted glass sconces dimly lit the entryway. On a sofa against the wall, men's and women's coats were piled haphazardly.

"I didn't know you had a dog," she said to Gisèle.

She led us into a large living room, its French windows opening onto a garden. From the next room, we heard the hubbub of conversation.

"I'm having some friends over for cards. But Jacques isn't here this evening . . ."

She didn't ask us to take off our coats. I sensed she was about to leave us in this room and go join the others.

"I'm not sure when he'll be back . . ."

There was an anxious expression in her eyes.

"Have you seen him today?" she asked Gisèle.

"Yes, we had lunch together. Mister Ansart took us to his restaurant."

The blonde woman's face relaxed.

"I didn't see him this morning . . . He went out very early . . ."

She was a pretty woman, but I remember that that evening she already seemed old to me, an adult my parents' age. I had felt something similar about Ansart. As for Jacques de Bavière, he reminded me of those young people who headed

off to fight in the Algerian War when I was six-
teen.

"You'll forgive me," she said, "but I have to
go rejoin my guests."

I glanced rapidly around the living room.
Sky-blue paneling, folding screen, pale marble
mantelpiece, mirrors. At the foot of a console
table, the carpet showed signs of intense wear,
and on one of the walls I noticed discoloration
where a painting had been removed. Behind the
French windows, bouquets of trees stood out in
the moonlight, and I couldn't see where the garden ended.

"It's like being in the country, isn't it?" the
blonde woman said to me, having followed my
gaze. "The garden stretches all the way to the
buildings on Rue de Berri . . ."

I felt like asking her point-blank if she was
really Jacques de Bavière's stepmother. She saw
us to the door.

"If I see Jacques, is there something you'd
like me to tell him?"

She had asked in a distracted voice, no doubt eager to return to her guests.

It was still early. People were lined up in front of the Normandie cinema for the second showing.

We walked down the avenue with the dog.

"Do you think she's really his stepmother?" I asked.

"That's what he says. He told me she runs a bridge club out of the apartment and he sometimes helps out."

A bridge club. That explained the feeling of unease I had experienced. I wouldn't have been surprised if the furniture was covered with slipcases. I had even noticed magazines piled up on a coffee table, like in a dentist's waiting room. So the apartment where Jacques de Bavière lived with his supposed stepmother was in fact nothing but a bridge club. I thought of my father. He too could easily have concocted a scheme like that, and Grabley would have acted as his secre-

tary and doorman. They really did all belong to
the same world.

We had reached the arcades of the Lido. I
was suddenly seized by a violent desire to flee
this city, as if I felt surrounded by a vague men-
ace.

"What's wrong? You're pale as a sheet . . ."

She had stopped walking. A group of strollers
jostled us as they went by. The dog, his head
raised toward us, seemed worried too.

"It's nothing . . . Just some passing dizzi-
ness . . ."

I forced a smile.

"Would you like to sit down for a bit, get
something to drink?"

She pointed toward a café, but I couldn't sit
in the middle of that Saturday evening crowd. I
would have suffocated. And anyway, there were
no free seats.

"No . . . Let's keep walking . . . I'll be fine . . ."

I took her hand.

"What would you say to leaving for Rome

right away?" I asked her. "Otherwise, I feel like it'll be too late . . ."

She looked at me, eyes wide.

"Why right away? We have to wait for Ansart and Jacques de Bavière to help us out . . . We can't do much of anything without them . . ."

"Well, what about crossing the street? It's quieter on the other side . . ."

And in fact, there were fewer people on the left-hand sidewalk. We walked toward Etoile, where we had parked the car. And today, trying to remember that evening, I see two silhouettes with a dog, walking up the avenue. Around them, the passersby become scarcer and scarcer, the cafés empty out, the movie houses go dark. In my dream, I was sitting that evening at a table on the Champs-Elysées amid several late-hour customers. They had already turned off the lights in the main room and the waiter was stacking the chairs as a hint that it was time for us to leave. I went out. I walked toward Etoile and heard a distant voice say: "We have to wait for Ansart and Jacques de Bavière to help us out . . ."—her voice, deep and always a little hoarse.

At Quai de Conti, the office windows were lit. Had Grabley forgotten to turn off the lights before going out on his rounds?

As we were crossing the darkened foyer with the dog, we heard laughter.

We tiptoed forward and Gisèle held the dog by his collar. We were hoping to slip by to the stairs without attracting any attention. But just as we passed by the half-open door of the office, it suddenly swung open and Grabley appeared, glass in hand.

He jumped when he saw us. He remained standing in the doorway, staring in surprise at the dog.

"Well, now . . . I don't believe I've met this one . . ."

Had he had too much to drink? With a ceremonial gesture, he ushered us in.

A small young woman with a round face and

short brown hair was sitting on the couch. At her feet was a bottle of champagne. She was holding a glass, and she didn't seem at all put out by our sudden appearance. Grabley introduced us.

"Sylvette . . . Obligado and Miss . . ."

She smiled at us.

"You might offer them some champagne," she said to Grabley. "I don't like drinking alone."

"I'll go fetch some glasses . . ."

But he didn't find any in the kitchen. There were only two left: his and the girl's. He would have to bring us teacups, or even those paper cups we'd been using for the past few weeks.

"No need," I told him.

The dog went toward the small brunette. Gisèle pulled him back by his collar.

"Let him go . . . I love dogs . . ."

She petted his forehead.

"Guess where I met Sylvette?" asked Grabley.

"Do you really think they're interested?" she said.

"I met her at the Tomate . . ."

Gisèle frowned. I was afraid she'd leave then and there.

The small brunette took a sip of champagne to hide her embarrassment.

"Do you know the Tomate, Obligado?"

I remembered walking past that establishment every Sunday evening on the way to picking up my mother, who was performing in a theater near Pigalle.

"I'm a dancer," she said sheepishly, "and they hired me for a two-week engagement . . . But I don't think I'll stay . . . The show is kind of creepy . . ."

"Not in the slightest," said Grabley.

She blushed and lowered her eyes.

It was ridiculous to feel self-conscious in front of us. I remembered those Sunday evenings when I crossed Paris on foot, from the Left Bank to Pigalle, and the neon sign at the end of Rue Notre-Dame-de-Lorette—red, then green, then blue.

LA TOMATE

CONTINUOUS

STRIPTEASE

A bit farther up was the Théâtre Fontaine. My mother was in a vaudeville show there: *The Perfumed Princess*. We would catch the last bus back to the Quai de Conti apartment, which was in almost as much disrepair then as now.

"To the Tomate!" said Grabley, raising his glass.

The small brunette raised hers as well, as if in defiance. Gisèle and I sat still. So did the dog. Their glasses clinked. There was a long silence. We were all under the wan light of the ceiling bulb, as if celebrating some mysterious birthday.

"Please excuse me," Gisèle said, "I'm dead on my feet."

"Tomorrow is Sunday, we can all go to the Tomate to watch Sylvette," Grabley said.

And once again, I thought of all those by-gone Sunday evenings.

* * *

I slept fitfully. Several times I awoke with a start, and reassured myself that she was still beside me in bed. I had a temperature. The room had turned into a train compartment. The silhouettes of Grabley and the small brunette appeared in the window frame. They were standing on the platform, waiting for us to depart. They were each holding a paper cup and they raised their arms in a toast, as if in slow motion. I could hear Grabley's half-muffled voice:

"We can all meet tomorrow at the Tomate . . ."

But I knew full well we wouldn't show up. We were leaving Paris for good. The train jerked to a start. The buildings and houses of the suburbs stood out one last time, black against a crepuscular sky. We were squeezed together in a couchette and the jostling carriage shook us violently. The next morning, the train would stop at a platform flooded in sunlight.

It was Sunday. We got up very late, feeling as if we had the flu. We had to find an open pharmacy in the neighborhood where we could buy some aspirin. And anyway, we needed to walk the dog.

Grabley had already gone out. He had left a note, lying conspicuously on the office couch.

My dear Obligado,

You aren't up yet, and I have to go to eleven o'clock Mass at Saint-Germain-des-Prés.

Your father called this morning, but I could barely hear him because he was calling from an outdoor phone booth: the car horns and traffic covered his voice.

On top of which, we were cut off, but I'm sure he'll call back. Life in Switzerland must not be easy for him. I tried to convince him not to go there. It can be a tough place if you don't have the cash . . .

We're expecting you this evening without fail, at the Tomate. The last two shows are at eight and ten-thirty. Take your pick.

Afterward, we're going to have a late supper in the neighborhood. I hope you can join us.
Henri

There was an open pharmacy on Rue Saint-André-des-Arts. We went to take the aspirin in a café on the quay, then walked to the Pont de la Tournelle after letting the dog off the leash.

It was nice out, as it had been the previous day, but colder, like a sunny day in February. Soon it would be spring. At least, I comforted myself with that illusion, as the prospect of spending the entire winter in Paris without knowing whether I could stay in the apartment made me uneasy.

As we walked, we began to feel better. We had lunch in a hotel on the Quai des Grands-Augustins called the Relais Bisson. When we saw how expensive the dishes were, we ordered just some soup, a dessert, and a little chopped meat for the dog.

And the afternoon drifted by in a gentle torpor on the bed in the fifth-floor bedroom, and, later, listening to the radio. We had plugged in the one in the office. I remember that it was a program about jazz musicians.

Suddenly, the charm evaporated: In an hour, we'd have to keep the appointment Ansart had set for us.

"How about if we just stood him up?" I asked.

She paused a moment. I could feel her giving in.

"If we do, we can never see them again, and we'd have to leave the car on Rue Raffet."

She took a cigarette from a pack of Camels that Grabley had left behind. She lit it and sucked in a puff. She coughed. It was the first time I'd ever seen her smoke.

"It would be stupid to break it off with them . . ."

I was disappointed that she'd changed her mind. She stubbed out her cigarette in the ashtray.

"We'll do what they want, and then I'll ask Ansart for a lot of money so we can go to Rome."

I had the impression she was only saying that

to mollify me and didn't really believe it. A last beam of sunlight bathed the tip of the Ile de la Cité, just at the end of the Vert-Galant park. There were only a few passersby left on the quay and the booksellers were closing their stalls. I heard the clock on the Institut chime five P.M.

We had decided to leave the dog in the apartment, intending to come back and get him as soon as we could. But the moment we shut the door, he started barking and whining incessantly, so we had to resign ourselves to taking him with us to the appointment.

It was still light when we arrived at the Bois de Boulogne. We were early, so we stopped in front of the old Château de Madrid. We walked in the clearing lined with umbrella pines up to the Saint-James pond, where I had watched the ice skaters one winter in my childhood. The smell of wet earth and the gathering dark again reminded me of bygone Sunday evenings, so much so that I felt the same muted anxiety as I used to feel at the thought of returning to boarding school the next morning. Of course, the situation was different now; I was walking in the Bois de Boulogne with her and not with my father, or with my pals Charell or Karvé. But something similar was hovering in the air, the same odor, and it was also a Sunday.

"Let's get going," she said.

She, too, looked anxious. To steady my nerves, I kept my eyes fixed on the dog running ahead of us. I asked whether we should take the car. She said it wasn't worth it.

We walked down Rue de la Ferme. Now she had the dog on a leash. We went past the entryway of the Charells' building, then past the Howlett riding stables, which looked abandoned. The Charells had surely moved away. They belonged to that category of people who never really settle anywhere. Where could Alain Charell have been this evening? Somewhere in Mexico? I heard a distant clacking of horseshoes. I turned around: two riders, visible only in silhouette, had just appeared at the end of the street. Was one of them the man we had to approach in a little while?

Gradually they moved closer to us. There was still time to turn back, take the car, leave it in front of the building on Rue Raffet, vanish with the dog and never be heard from again.

She gave my arm a tight squeeze.

"This won't take long," she said.

"You think so?"

"Once we've talked to this guy, we leave the café and let them sort out the rest themselves."

The two riders had turned right, into narrow Rue Saint-James. The clacking of horseshoes faded away.

We had reached the café. Farther on, in the part of Rue de la Ferme nearer the Seine, I noticed Ansart's car. Someone was sitting on one of the fenders. Jacques de Bavière? I wasn't sure. Two silhouettes occupied the front seats.

We went in. I was surprised by how fancy the place was: I'd expected just a simple café. A bar and round tables made of mahogany. Armchairs of slightly worn leather. Wood paneling on the walls. In the brick fireplace, they had lit a fire.

We took our seats at the table closest to the door. Around us were a few patrons, but I didn't recognize our man among them.

The dog had lain down submissively at our feet. We ordered two coffees and I paid the check, so that we could leave as soon as we had delivered our message to the unknown man.

Gisèle pulled Grabley's cigarettes from the pocket of her raincoat and lit one. She inhaled, clumsily. Her hand was shaking.

I asked:

"Are you afraid?"

"Not at all."

The door opened and three people walked in, a woman and two men. One of them was definitely the man in the photo: wide forehead, very dark hair, brushed back.

They were having a lively conversation. The woman burst out laughing.

They sat at a table in back, near the fireplace. The man had removed his navy blue overcoat. He was not wearing riding breeches.

Gisèle stubbed out her cigarette in the ashtray. She was looking down. Was she trying to avoid the man's eyes?

He was facing us, over there, at the table in back. The other two, a brunette of about thirty and a blond man with a narrow face and aquiline nose, were in profile.

The woman had a loud voice. The man seemed younger than on the enlarged identity photo.

I stood up, my palms moist.

I moved forward. I was standing next to their table. They stopped talking.

I leaned toward him:

"I have a message for you."

"A message from whom?"

He had a high-pitched voice, as if strangled, and he seemed annoyed that I should come bother him.

"From Pierre Ansart. He's waiting for you in the car on the corner."

I stood stiffly, straining to articulate the syllables as clearly as possible.

"Ansart?"

His face expressed the discomfiture of someone being reprimanded when and where he least expected it.

"He wants to see me right now?"

"Yes."

He glanced anxiously toward the entrance.

"Excuse me for a moment," he said to his two companions. "I just have to go say hello to a friend who's waiting outside."

The other two gave me a condescending once-over: was it because of my extreme youth and careless attire? It occurred to me that I could be identified later. Had they noticed Gisèle's presence?

He stood up and slipped on his navy blue overcoat. He turned toward the blond man and said:

"Book a table for tonight . . . There'll be eight of us . . ."

"That's silly," the woman said. "We could have dinner at my place . . ."

"Nonsense . . . Back in a minute . . ."

I remained standing firmly in front of them. He said to me:

"So where is this car?"

"I'll show you."

I walked ahead of him to the exit. Gisèle was waiting, standing by our table with the dog. He seemed surprised by her presence. I held the door and let the two of them pass.

The car pulled up. They had parked on the corner of Rue de Longchamp. Jacques de Bavière was standing, leaning slightly against the carriage. Ansart got out, leaving the front door open, and waved his arm at us. The street was brightly lit. In the cold, limpid air, the car stood out starkly against the building façades and sections of wall.

The man walked toward them, and we remained in place on the sidewalk. He had forgotten us. He, too, raised his arm, waving at Ansart.

He said:

"This is a surprise . . ."

He and Ansart chatted in the middle of the street. We could only hear the murmur of their voices. We could have joined them. It would only have taken a few steps. But I sensed that if we went toward them, we would be entering a danger zone. Besides, neither Ansart nor Jacques de Bavière was paying us the slightest attention. Suddenly, they were far away, in another space—I'd say, in another time—and today that scene has frozen forever.

Even the dog, which wasn't on its leash, stood still, at our sides, as if he, too, could sense an invisible boundary between them and us.

Jacques de Bavière opened one of the rear doors and let the man get in, then sat next to him. Ansart took his seat in front. The one at the wheel hadn't left the car and I couldn't make out his face. The doors shut. The car made a U-turn and headed down Rue de la Ferme toward the Seine.

I watched it go until it disappeared around the corner of the quay.

I asked Gisèle:

"Where do you think they're going?"

"They're taking him to Rue Raffet . . ."

"But he told his friends he'd be right back . . ."

And yet, they hadn't forced him into the car.

It was probably Ansart who had persuaded him to go with them, during their brief conversation in the middle of the street.

"Maybe I should go tell the other two not to wait," I said.

"No . . . Let's not get mixed up in this . . ."

I was surprised by her categorical tone, and I got the distinct impression she knew more than I did.

"You really think we shouldn't tell them?"

"No, of course not . . . They won't trust us . . . and they'll ask questions . . ."

I pictured myself standing next to their table, explaining that their friend had left in a car. And the questions would rain down like blows, increasingly numerous and insistent:

You're sure you saw him leave? Who with?

Who gave you this message?

Where do these people live?

Who are you, anyway?

And I, unable to flee the avalanche of their questions, my legs leaden as in a nightmare.

"We shouldn't stay here," I said to her.

They could have come out at any moment to look for their friend. We took Rue de la Ferme toward the Bois. As we passed by the Charells' old building, I wondered what Alain would have thought of all this.

I felt uneasy. A man had taken his leave of two people, saying he'd be "back in a minute." Instead, he had been made to get in a car that had headed off toward the Seine. We were, she and I, witnesses but also accessories to this disappearance. It had all happened in a street in Neuilly, near the Bois de Boulogne, a neighborhood that reminded me of other Sundays . . . I used to walk in the alleys of the Bois with my father and one of his friends, a very tall, thin man, who had retained, from a time of former prosperity, only a fur coat and a blazer, which he wore according to the season. At the time, I had noticed how threadbare his clothes were. We would walk him home in the evening, to his hotel in Neuilly that looked like a boardinghouse. His room, he said, was small but adequate.

"What are you thinking about?"

She had taken my arm. We skirted the clearing with the umbrella pines. Had we bisected it, we would have arrived faster at the place where the car was parked. But it was too dark and only Boulevard Richard-Wallace was lit.

I was thinking about that man's outline, his smile and well-preserved face. But after a while, you noticed that he had become one with the threadbare blazer and fur coat, and that his spirit was broken. Who was he? What had become of him? He had certainly disappeared, just like that other man, a little while ago.

She started the car and we drove toward the Jardin d'Acclimatation. I looked at the lights in the apartment windows.

She had stopped at a red light on Avenue de Madrid. She was frowning. She seemed to be feeling the same unease as I was.

The building façades paraded by. It was a shame we didn't know anyone there. We could have knocked at one of those quiet apartments. We would have been invited in to dinner, along with distinguished and reassuring company. I remembered what the man had said:

"Book a table for tonight . . . There'll be eight of us . . ."

Had they made the reservation anyway, after vainly waiting for his return? In that case, the seven guests had gathered and were still waiting for the eighth to show. But the chair would remain empty.

A restaurant open on Sunday evening . . . We used to go to one, my father, his friend, and I, near Place de l'Etoile. We would go early, around seven-thirty. The diners would start arriving when we had finished eating. One Sunday evening, a group of very elegant people came in and, even at age eleven, I had been dazzled by the beauty and vivaciousness of the women. The gaze of one of them suddenly fell on my father's friend. He was wearing his threadbare blazer. She appeared stunned to see him there, but after a moment her face regained its smooth composure. She went to join her dinner companions at a table far from ours.

He, on the other hand, had grown very pale. He leaned toward my father and said something that has been etched in my memory:

"Gaëlle just went by . . . I recognized her immediately . . . But I've changed so much since the war . . ."

We had reached the Porte Maillot. She turned to me.

"Where do you feel like going?"

"I have no idea . . ."

We both felt disoriented, helpless. Should we go to Ansart's to find out what had happened? But it wasn't really our business. I would have preferred never to see those people again and to get out of Paris right away.

"Now's when we should leave for Rome," I said to her.

"Sure, but we don't have enough money."

I had on me the seven thousand five hundred francs that Dell'Aversano had given me, plus the four thousand from Ansart. It was more than enough. I didn't dare ask how much money she had.

I repeated that I'd been promised a steady job in Rome and that we wouldn't have any problems. I ended up persuading her.

"We'll have to bring the dog," she said.

"Of course . . ."

After a moment's reflection, she added:

"The easiest way would be to go in this car. Even if we don't ask them, they could hardly file a complaint . . ."

She laughed, a nervous laugh. Indeed, they wouldn't file a complaint because this evening we had become their accomplices and they were dependent on our silence. The thought sent a chill up my spine. I was the one who had said, "I have a message for you from Pierre Ansart. He's waiting for you in the car on the corner." And in front of two witnesses. And I'd taken money for it.

I must have had a strange expression on my face, because she put her arm around my shoulder and I felt her lips brush my cheek.

"Don't you worry about a thing," she murmured in my ear.

"Shall we go see Grabley . . . ? At around nine, he'll be at the Tomate . . ."

There was something homey and reassuring about the sound of the word "Tomate."

"If you want . . ."

Naturally, I wasn't expecting any moral support from Grabley. He had something in common with my father: they both wore suits, ties, and shoes like everyone else. They spoke unaccented French, smoked cigarettes, drank espresso, and ate oysters. But when in their company, you were seized by doubt and you felt like touching them, the way you rub cloth between your fingers, to make sure they really existed.

"Do you think he can do anything for us?" she asked.

"Who knows?"

It was too early to go meet him. We still had two hours to kill. On the left, just nearby, on the avenue, I noticed the lit façade of the Maillot Palace cinema, and I suggested we go see the film they were showing: *Cattle Queen of Montana*. The usherette didn't say a word about the dog.

Once we'd settled into the red velvet seats, my uneasiness dissipated.

Rue Notre-Dame-de-Lorette was dark and the sidewalks deserted. At that hour, people were finishing their dinner and going to bed early. Tomorrow would be another day of school and work. Up above, the Tomate's neon sign shone to no purpose in a dead street. Who would be there to watch the Sunday night show? A sailor on shore leave, before heading back to the Gare Saint-Lazare to catch the Cherbourg train?

The usherette pointed the way backstage. The dressing rooms were in the basement. We went down a flight of stairs leading to a small lounge, its walls decorated with old posters from the place.

Grabley was standing by one of the dressing room doors, wearing a glen plaid suit and a suede tie. He looked worried.

"What a nice surprise . . . It was good of you to come . . ."

But he confided to us that Sylvette was in a

very bad mood. She was in her dressing room, changing. We'd made the right choice coming when we did, as there would be no ten-thirty performance. He suggested we go find our seats. I answered that we were happier staying there with him. Besides, they wouldn't let us in the auditorium with the dog.

"Too bad for you."

He was visibly offended by our lack of enthusiasm for the show.

The dressing room door opened and Sylvette appeared. She was wearing a black domino and leopard-skin basque. She greeted us curtly. Then, turning to Grabley, she told him he was under no obligation to hang around the wings waiting for her. She was mortified enough being in this show, but having someone hovering around her all the time, even in her dressing room, only made it worse . . . The discussion got heated. Yes, any man with half a brain would have understood it was humiliating for a dancer to demean herself like this, but she had to make a living, and it wasn't like anybody was going

to help her. Then she chided him for bringing
us here. She hadn't *entirely* turned into a circus
animal or some beast you go visit in the zoo on
Sundays. Grabley lowered his eyes. She ditched
us there and headed to the staircase, which she
started to climb in her high heels, and the sway-
ing of her hips immediately reminded me of
something. Of course! The naked girl with her
hair tied back in a ponytail, in one of the magazines in the office—that was she.

Grabley gazed after her until she was gone.
The first bars of a Mexican tune blared out from
trumpets. No doubt she had just gone onstage.

"She can be so hard," he said, "so hard . . ."

Gisèle and I exchanged a look and could
barely keep from laughing. Fortunately, he
wasn't paying us any attention. He was staring
at the top of the stairs, looking numb, as if she
had left for good.

After a while, we weren't sure whether we
should stay or not. And I didn't feel like laughing anymore. Was it because of the yellow light
in the lounge, the old posters on the walls indi-

cating that this had once been a proper caba-
ret, the Mexican trumpets, this man dressed in
his glen plaid suit and suede tie who had just
been snapped at? A diffuse melancholy floated
over us.

Once more, I thought of my father. I imagined him in the same situation, wearing his navy
blue coat and waiting at the dressing room door
in a place very much like this: some "Kit Cat" or
"Carrousel" in Geneva or Lausanne. I remembered the last Christmas we spent together. I was
fifteen. He had come to collect me in a boarding
school in the Haute-Savoie where they couldn't
keep me over the holidays.

A woman was waiting for him in Geneva,
twenty years younger than he, an Italian with
straw-blond hair, and the three of us took the
plane for Rome. From that trip, there remains a
photograph that I rediscovered thirty years later,
at the bottom of a trunk full of papers. It has
captured forever the image of a New Year's Eve
celebration in a nightclub near the Via Veneto,
where the Italian woman had dragged us after

making a scene with my father: you could hear the shouting in the hotel corridor.

We are sitting before a champagne bucket. Several couples are dancing behind us. Around the table, a man with dark hair, slicked back; his face wears an expression of forced gaiety. Next to him, a woman of about thirty, lots of foundation, very frizzy straw-blond hair tied in a bun. And a teenager with a rented tux that is too big for him and a blank look on his face, like all children who find themselves in bad company because they don't have any say and can't yet live their lives. If I wanted to return to Rome, it was to erase that past.

"Want to go?" Gisèle asked me.

The dog was getting restless. He had climbed the stairs, then, realizing we weren't following, had come back down and settled at the foot of the staircase.

Grabley suddenly emerged from his dejection:

"You aren't leaving, are you? Sylvette will be

so disappointed . . . And she'll give me an even harder time . . ."

But I felt no pity for him. He reminded me of my father, the woman's straw-blond hair, and that New Year's Eve. These days I was free to come and go as I pleased.

"We can't stay, old man," I said. "I have to take Gisèle home to Saint-Leu-la-Forêt."

"You really don't want to have a late supper with us?"

He was wearing the same anxious expression as my father had had on that sidewalk on the Via Veneto. In front of us, a group of revelers were tooting little party horns. The woman with the straw-blond hair seemed to be sulking. Suddenly she started walking quickly, then running, as if she wanted to lose us. My father said to me:

"Quick . . . Catch her . . . be nice to her . . . Tell her how much we love her . . . that we need her . . . Give her this . . ."

And he slipped me a small box wrapped in silver paper.

I had run. I was too young at the time. And now I felt a kind of sadness mixed with indifference for that still recent past. None of it mattered anymore. Not my father, not Grabley, not that fellow they had taken away in the car earlier. They could all go to hell.

On the sidewalk, I felt lighter, removed from everything. I wished she could have shared my state of mind. I put my arm around her shoulder and we walked to the car.

The dog went ahead of us. I suggested we leave for Rome right away. But she had left her money in one of the suitcases.

All we had to do was stop by Quai de Conti and stash the suitcases in the trunk of the car.

"Up to you," she said.

She had become carefree again, like me.

But a thought brought me back to reality. I was underage and I had to get hold of an authorization form to travel abroad, at the bottom of which I'd forge my father's signature. I didn't dare tell her.

"Actually, we can't leave this evening," I said. "First that Italian has to give me all the information."

The theater on Rue Fontaine was closed. A few scattered lights toward the top of the building. After following the neighborhood streets haphazardly, we stopped in front of a restaurant, the Gavarny.

We had dinner there. At first, I was afraid Grabley and Sylvette might show up, but I told myself they preferred noisier places. I recognized the man in the white jacket who served us, from the rare times I used to eat there with my mother, on Sunday evenings after her performance.

When we walked in, he was sitting at a table doing a crossword puzzle. I wondered if the music was coming from a speaker at the back of the room or from a radio: music with the lunar sound of a hammered dulcimer.

The dog stretched out at my feet. I petted him to reassure myself he was really there. I was sitting across from her. I didn't take my eyes off her. I ran my hand over her face. Once again, I felt a stab of fear that she would vanish.

As of that evening, we had cut all our ties. Nothing around us was real anymore. Not Grabley, not my father lost in Switzerland, not my mother, somewhere in the south of Spain, not those people I had met and about whom I knew nothing: Ansart, Jacques de Bavière . . . The restaurant dining room was also stripped of any reality, like one of those places you frequented long ago and revisit in a dream.

After leaving the Gavarny, my mother and I used to take the number 67 bus at Place Pigalle, which dropped us off at the Quai du Louvre. Just three years since then, and already it was another lifetime . . . Only the man in the white jacket remained at his post. I would have liked to talk to him, but what could he have told me?

"Pinch me so I know I'm not dreaming . . ."

She pinched my cheek.

"Harder."

She burst out laughing. And her laugh echoed

in the empty dining room. I asked if she, too, felt as if she were in a dream.

"Yes, sometimes."

The man in the white jacket had plunged back in to his crossword puzzle. There wouldn't be any more customers tonight.

She had taken my hand and was looking at me with her pale blue eyes, smiling.

She raised her hand and pinched my cheek, even harder than the other times.

"Wake up . . ."

The man stood up from his chair and went to turn on the radio behind the bar. A musical theme, then the voice of an announcer reading a news bulletin. I could make out only the timbre of the voice, like background noise.

"So, are you awake?"

"I'm not sure," I said. "I'd rather keep it vague."

On Sunday evenings, in the boarding school dormitory after our return from holidays, the proctor would turn out the lights at a quarter to nine and it would take a while for sleep to come.

I would wake with a start during the night, not knowing where I was. The night-light bathing the rows of bunks in a bluish glow yanked me back to reality. And since that time, whenever I've dreamed, I've tried to hold off the moment of waking for fear of finding myself back in that dormitory. I tried to explain this to her.

"Me too," she said, "that often happens to me . . . I'm afraid of waking up in jail . . ."

I asked her why in jail? But she seemed embarrassed, and finally answered:

"That's just how it is . . ."

Outside, I paused. Going back to the Quai de Conti just seemed too tedious. I would have preferred for us to be in a place that didn't trigger any past associations. But she said none of that mattered, as long as we were together.

We drive down Rue Blanche. Once more, I feel like I'm in a dream. And in this dream, I experience a sensation of euphoria. The car glides along without my hearing the sound of the engine, as if it were coasting down the slope in idle.

On Avenue de l'Opéra, the lights and empty street open before us. She turns toward me:

"We can leave tomorrow, if you like."

For the first time in my life, I feel as if the obstacles and constraints holding me back have been removed. Perhaps this is just an illusion that will evaporate tomorrow morning. I lower the window and the cold air heightens my euphoria. Not the slightest fog, the slightest halo around the streetlamps sparkling down the avenue.

We cross the Pont du Carrousel and, in my memory, we follow the quay against traffic, ignoring the one-way signs; we pass by the Pont des Arts, driving slowly, with no cars coming in the opposite direction.

Grabley isn't there yet. We cross through the foyer and the apartment detaches itself from the past. I enter it for the first time. It's she who guides me. Ahead of me she climbs the small staircase leading to the fifth floor. In the bedroom, we don't put on the light.

The lamps along the quay project a beam of light on the ceiling as bright as the kind that, in summer, filters through the slats of the venetian blinds. She is stretched out on the bed, in her black skirt and pullover.

The next morning, when we left the apartment, Grabley still hadn't come back. We had decided to return the car to Ansart and never see them again, him and Jacques de Bavière. We planned to leave for Rome as soon as possible.

We tried calling them, but no one answered the phone at Ansart's, nor at Jacques de Bavière's supposed residence. Too bad. We were leaning toward just abandoning the car on Rue Raffet.

It was a sunny autumn day, like the day before. I felt a sense of lightness and well-being at the thought of our departure. I would be leaving behind only things that were starting to fall apart: Grabley, the empty apartment . . . I just needed to find the authorization form I had used the previous year for a trip to Belgium, and I'd alter the date and destination. In Rome, I could certainly manage to avoid the French authorities and my draft obligations.

She told me there was no problem with her

leaving France. I tried to find out more about this husband she'd mentioned.

She hadn't seen him in a long time—nearly three months by now. She had gotten married on a whim. But who was he, exactly?

She looked me in the eye with a tight smile and said:

"Oh, kind of a strange guy . . . He runs a circus . . ."

I wasn't sure if she was joking or telling the truth.

She seemed to be watching for my reaction.

"A circus?"

"Yes, a circus . . ."

He had left on tour with the circus, but she hadn't wanted to go with him.

"I don't like talking about this . . ."

And there was silence between us all the way until we arrived at the building on Rue Raffet.

We rang at the door of the apartment. No one answered.

"They might be at the restaurant," said Gisèle.

A woman was staring at us, at the entrance to the courtyard. She walked up to us.

"Are you looking for somebody?"

Her tone was curt, as if she were suspicious of us.

"Mister Ansart," Gisèle said.

"Mister Ansart left very early this morning. He gave me the keys to his apartment. He won't be back for at least three months."

So this was the concierge.

"He didn't say where he was going?" asked Gisèle.

"No."

"And there's no place we can write to him?"

"He said he'd send me his new address. If you want to write him, you can leave the letter with me."

Her tone had softened a bit. She watched after us as we crossed back through the courtyard with the dog. She seemed to find "Mister Ansart's" departure perfectly normal. Eventually, she would ask herself about that man who seemed so pleasant and well-mannered. After that, others would ask, perhaps in the same office where Gisèle and I had been questioned. They would ask her to remember the smallest details about Ansart, who came to visit him. And she would remember that soon after his disappearance, a young man and young woman with a dog had rung at the apartment.

"What should we do with the car?" I asked Gisèle.

"We'll keep it."

She rummaged in the glove compartment and pulled out the registration. It was in the name of Pierre Louis Ansart, born January 22, 1921, in Paris 10th, residing 14 Rue Raffet, Paris 16th.

We skirted the Bois de Boulogne, by the same route we'd taken on Saturday to go have lunch in Ansart's restaurant. I held onto his registration card. We turned onto Rue des Belles-Feuilles. The restaurant was closed. They had nailed wooden panels onto the façade, with peeling green paint that surely dated from the time when the Belles Feuilles was, as Ansart had said, a working-class café.

Now she seemed concerned. There must have been a connection between Ansart's sudden disappearance and the incident in Neuilly the day before, in which we had been more than just bystanders.

"Do you think Jacques de Bavière has also taken off?" I asked.

She shrugged. I recalled Martine's face, the way she had waved to us as we walked across the courtyard the other night.

"What about Martine? Can we reach her somewhere?"

She knew almost nothing about Martine, other than that she had been living with Ansart for several years. The only thing she remembered was her name: Martine Gaul.

We ended up in a café on Rue Spontini, where we ordered two sandwiches and two glasses of orange juice. She took a small address book from her bag and asked me to call Rue Washington to see whether Jacques de Bavière was still there.

"Hello . . . Who's this?"

A woman with a deep voice. The one who had greeted us on Saturday evening?

"I'd like to speak with Jacques de Bavière, please . . ."

"Who are you?"

Her tone was sharp, the tone of someone on the alert.

"We're friends of Jacques. We came over on Saturday . . ."

"Jacques has left for Belgium."

"Will he be gone long?"

"I couldn't say."

"Did Mister Ansart go with him?"

There was a moment's pause. I even thought the line had gone dead.

"I don't know the person you mean. I'm very sorry, but I have to go now."

She hung up.

So they had both gone. With Martine, no doubt. To Belgium, or somewhere else. How could we find out?

"Are you sure his name is de Bavière?" I asked Gisèle.

"Yes, de Bavière."

What good would that do us? He surely wasn't in the phone book, or in the social register, as his name might imply.

She said she wanted to try somewhere else, where we might stand a better chance of finding out news of Ansart. We followed the major boulevards. She didn't offer any explanations. When we arrived at Place de la République, we took Boulevard du Temple, then stopped in a street that ran parallel to it, slightly downhill. In front of us was the Winter Circus.

She pointed out a café farther down the road, about fifty yards away.

"Go in and ask the guy behind the bar if he has any news of Mister Ansart . . ."

Why wasn't she coming with me?

I walked down the street, turning around to make sure she was still there. I thought she might wait for me to enter the café, then vanish like all the others.

The café didn't display any name, but an ad for Belgian beer was stickered on the façade. I went in. At the back of a small room were a few tables where patrons were having lunch.

Behind the bar stood a tall, dark-haired man with a slightly squashed nose wearing a dark blue suit; he was on the phone. I waited. A waiter in a burgundy jacket came up to me.

"A bottle of Vittel."

The phone conversation dragged on. The man listened to his correspondent and occasionally answered, "Yes . . . yes . . . all right . . ." or gave a brief grunt of assent. He had jammed the receiver between his shoulder and cheek to light a cigarette and his eyes met mine, but I don't know if he really saw me. He hung up.

I asked him in a timid voice:

"Do you have any news of Mister Ansart?"

He smiled at me. But I could tell this smile was just a façade, a way of establishing distance between us.

"You know Mister Ansart?"

His voice had a childlike timbre that reminded me of the actor Jean Marais. He came around the bar to join me on the other side and leaned on it with his elbow.

"Yes, I know him, and I also know Martine Gaul."

Why had I added that detail? To make him trust me?

"I went by Rue Raffet this morning and they were gone."

He looked me over with a benevolent eye, still with that smile. The elegant cut of his suit and his voice clashed with the surroundings. Was he really the owner of this café?

"They're gone, but they will certainly be back. That's all I can tell you."

He smile widened, and the look in his eyes made it clear that, indeed, he wouldn't say any more.

I went to pay for the bottle of Vittel, but he waved his hand.

"No . . . Forget it . . ."

He opened the door for me himself and gave me a brief nod of farewell. He was still smiling.

In the car, Gisèle asked:

"What did he say?"

She must have known that man with his immutable smile. She had no doubt met him with Ansart and Jacques de Bavière.

"He said they would certainly be back, but he didn't seem to want to provide any details."

"It doesn't matter. In any case, we'll never see them again. We'll be in Rome."

We followed the boulevard up to Place de la Bastille. We weren't far from Dell'Aversano's shop. I suggested that we stop in to finalize our travel arrangements.

"Had you been in that café before?" I asked Gisèle.

"Yes. Lots of times."

She paused, then said, as if reluctantly:

"It was when my husband worked at the Winter Circus."

She fell silent. I thought of the man in the dark blue suit. His smile had impressed me and I still remembered it ten years later, when one afternoon I happened to find myself near the

Winter Circus. I hadn't been able to resist going into that café. It was around 1973.

He was standing behind the bar, less elegant than the first time, features drawn and hair gone gray. A number of photos were glued to the wall, some of them signed, depicting performers from the Winter Circus who patronized the café.

One of the photos, larger than the others, had caught my eye. It showed a whole group of people standing at the bar, around a blonde woman wearing a rider's jacket. And among them, I recognized Gisèle.

I had ordered a bottle of Vittel, like the first time.

At that hour of the afternoon, he and I were the only ones there. I asked him point blank:

"Did you know that girl?"

I joined him behind the bar and pointed out Gisèle in the photo. He didn't seem the least bit surprised by my actions.

He leaned closer to the picture.

"Oh, sure, I knew her . . . She was really young . . . She used to spend her evenings here

. . . Her husband worked for the circus . . . She would wait for him . . . She always looked bored . . . That must be a good ten years ago . . ."

"But what did her husband do, exactly?"

"He must have been part of the circus staff. He was older than her."

I sensed that he'd answer any question I asked. I was still young at the time and had a shy, polite air about me. And he, no doubt, wanted nothing better than to chat away the empty hours of that early summer afternoon.

He seemed much more accessible than he had ten years earlier. He had lost his mystery, or rather the mystery I'd lent him. The slim man in the dark blue suit was nothing more today than a café proprietor on Rue Amelot, practically your basic barkeep.

"Did you know Pierre Ansart?"

He cast me a surprised glance and once again I saw on his face the disingenuous smile from before.

"How come? Did *you* know Pierre?"

"That girl introduced me to him about ten years ago."

He knitted his brow.

"The girl in the photo? . . . Pierre must have met her here . . . He often came to see me . . ."

"And what about a younger man named Jacques de Bavière, does that ring a bell?"

"No."

"He was a friend of Ansart's."

"I didn't know all of Pierre's friends . . ."

"You don't know what became of him, do you?"

Again that smile.

"Pierre? No. He's not in Paris anymore, that much I know."

I stopped talking. I was waiting for him to say what he'd told me the first time: They're gone, but they will certainly be back.

Through the half-open door, the sun threw bright spots on the walls and empty tables in back.

"So, you were a close friend of Ansart's?"

His eyes and face took on a sarcastic expression.

"We met in 1943. And that same year, we both got sent to Poissy prison . . . As you see, this all goes back a while . . ."

I remained silent. He added:

"But don't hold it against us. Anyone can make mistakes when they're young . . ."

I felt like telling him I'd already come here ten years earlier to ask for news of Ansart and that he hadn't wanted to tell me. Back then, there were still secrets to keep.

But now, these were all bygones, of no further importance.

"And are you still in touch with the girl?"

I was so startled by his question that I stammered a vague reply. Once alone, on the boulevard, I stupidly broke down in sobs.

We reached the Seine and followed the Quai des Célestins. Rummaging in my pocket for a pack of cigarettes, I realized I'd kept Ansart's registration card.

"Can you really depend on this guy we're going to see?" asked Gisèle.

"Yes. I believe he genuinely cares about me."

Indeed, thinking about it today, I can better appreciate Dell'Aversano's kindness toward me. He had been moved by my family situation, if such an adjective can be used when your parents completely neglect you. The first time I'd visited him, he had asked some questions about my studies and counseled me to keep at them, no doubt judging that a teenager left to his own devices would come to a bad end. According to him, I deserved better than to fence stolen furniture to some Saint-Paul junk dealer. I had admitted that I dreamed of becoming a writer and had favorably impressed him when I said my bedside companion was a volume of Stendhal's correspondence called *To the Happy Few*.

He was sitting at his desk at the back of the shop. He looked at Gisèle and the dog in surprise.

I introduced Gisèle as my sister.

"I have all your information for you," he said.

My job in Rome with his fellow bookseller didn't start for another two months.

"Why, had you wanted to leave right away?"

I didn't dare tell him that we had use of a car, or I'd have had to show him Ansart's registration and explain the whole story. Perhaps another time . . . But I did admit that I wanted to go there with Gisèle. Did he really believe she was my sister? I didn't read any sign of disapproval on his face. He simply turned to her:

"Are you prepared to find work in Rome?"

He asked her age. She told him she was twenty-one. He knew how old I was, and I dug my nails into my palms for fear he'd mention it in front of Gisèle.

"I even know your new address down there . . . If you like, I'll ask my friend if you can move in early . . ."

I thanked him. Would it be possible for my sister to live there with me?

He looked at the two of us more closely. I guessed that he was trying to find a physical resemblance between us and couldn't.

"That depends," he said. "Does your sister know how to type?"

"Yes," said Gisèle.

I was sure she was lying. I really couldn't picture her sitting at a typewriter.

"My friend will need someone who can type in French . . . I'll call him this evening to find out more about it."

He stood up and invited us to go have coffee. We walked by the car, but I didn't say anything and Gisèle was my accomplice in silence. Tomorrow, without fail, I'd tell him everything that had happened. I didn't have the right to hide anything from this man who had been so good to us.

He asked how much longer I could stay in the Quai de Conti apartment.

"Not more than three weeks . . ."

He couldn't understand how a father and mother could abandon a boy who was so passionate about literature and whose bedside book was called *To the Happy Few*. And what astounded him even more was that I considered my parents' attitude entirely natural, and that it had never even occurred to me to expect any help from them.

"So, you have to be settled in Rome three weeks from now and your sister has to be able to live with you . . ."

From the way he had pronounced the words *your sister*, I could tell he wasn't fooled.

"Does your sister like literature as much as you?"

Gisèle looked embarrassed. In the time we'd known each other, we had never once talked about books.

"I'm making her read *To the Happy Few*," I said.

"And do you like it?" Dell'Aversano asked.

"Very much."

She flashed him a winning smile. It was sunny

out and the air was warm for the season. We sat at the only sidewalk table left at the café. The clock on the church of Saint-Gervais chimed noon.

"So you know our future address in Rome?" I asked.

Dell'Aversano pulled an envelope from the inside pocket of his jacket.

"It's number 7 on Via Frescobaldi."

He turned to Gisèle:

"Do you know Rome?"

"No," Gisèle said.

"So then you weren't with your brother when he celebrated New Year's Eve there at age fifteen?"

He smiled at her and she smiled back.

"And this Via Frescobaldi," I asked, "what neighborhood is it in?"

"Here, I'll show you."

Using a ballpoint pen, he drew two parallel lines on the envelope.

"This is the Via Veneto . . . You do know the Via Veneto . . ."

I had told him the story of how, on my father's orders, I'd tried to catch the woman with straw-blond hair and too much foundation who was running away from us.

"You follow Via Pinciana past the gardens of the Villa Borghese . . ."

He continued drawing lines on the envelope and with the tip of his pen he showed us the way.

"You make a left, still skirting the Villa Borghese, and you come to Via Frescobaldi . . . And there it is . . ."

He drew a cross.

"The great thing about the neighborhood is that you're surrounded by green . . . Your street is right near the botanical gardens . . ."

Neither of us could take our eyes off the map he'd just sketched. I was walking with Gisèle, in summer, beneath the shade trees of Via Frescobaldi.

At Quai de Conti, Grabley had left a note on the office couch:

My dear Obligado,

Someone called for you around 2 P.M. A man claiming to be from the police. He left his name, Samson, and a number where you can reach him: TURBIGO 92-00.

I hope you haven't done something foolish.

Last night, the evening ended better than I expected and we were sorry you weren't with us. Would you like to join us again this evening, at the Tomate, for the 10:30 show?

Yours, Grabley

I asked Gisèle whether I should phone right away to find out what the man wanted. But we decided he should be the one to call back.

The afternoon was spent waiting, and the two of us did our best to overcome our nervousness. I had crumpled and torn up Grabley's note on which he'd written, "I hope you haven't done something foolish."

"You think they could know what we did yesterday afternoon?"

Gisèle shrugged and smiled at me. She seemed calmer than I was. We spread out the map of Rome on the floor and tried to familiarize ourselves with our new neighborhood, memorizing the names of the streets, monuments, and churches that were near our new home: Porta Pinciana, Santa Teresa, the Temple of Aesculapius, the Colonial Museum . . . No one would ever find us there.

Later, darkness began to fall and we were lying on the couch. She got up and put on her black skirt and pullover.

"I'm going out for cigarettes."

She wanted me to stay in case the phone rang. I asked her to buy the evening paper.

I watched her from the window. She didn't take the car. She walked with a languid step, hands in the pockets of her raincoat that she'd left unbuttoned.

She disappeared around the corner of the Hôtel des Monnaies.

I lay back down on the couch. I tried to recall the furniture that used to be in this office.

The telephone rang. A muffled, slightly drawling voice.

"I'm calling on behalf of Mister Samson, who asked you some questions last Thursday. A young girl was called in just after you . . . The two of you met up later at the Soleil-d'Or café."

He paused. But I didn't say anything. I felt incapable of uttering a single word.

"You have spent the last four days together and she is living at your address . . . I'm calling to warn you . . ."

The office was now half in shadow and he continued speaking in his muffled voice.

"There is a lot you don't know about this person . . . I suppose she even lied to you about her name . . . Her real name is Suzanne Kraay . . ."

He spelled out the name, mechanically: K-R-A-A-Y. It felt as if the voice I was hearing was prerecorded, like the talking clock.

"She has already committed several offenses that landed her in La Petite-Roquette for a few months . . . But I don't imagine she told you any of that . . . She probably also didn't tell you she's married . . ."

"I'm aware," I said, in a voice I tried to make curt.

There was a pause.

"You are certainly not aware of everything."

"I'm not interested," I told him.

"But I *am* interested, and you're forgetting that you're still a minor . . ."

Once again the voice was muffled, distant.

"And you're running a huge risk . . ."

I heard the crackling of static, as if my caller were standing at the far end of the world. Then the noise stopped and his voice came through, very near and distinct.

"I'd like to give you a quick rundown so that we can clear the air. It's in your interest. You should know what you're exposing yourself to, since you're a minor . . . Will you agree to meet me?"

He had spoken that last sentence in the tone,

at once obsequious and authoritarian, used by certain boarding school supervisors.

"All right," I said.

"This evening, ten o'clock, near your building . . . In the café on the quay, opposite the Louvre Colonnade . . . You can see it from your windows . . . I'll expect you at ten . . . I'm Mister Guélin."

He spelled his name, then hung up.

I hung up in turn. Before he'd introduced himself, his voice had reminded me of a man I used to run into on Saturdays, when I went to the Jardin du Luxembourg or the Danton cinema. He always wore a gray sweat suit and had just come from the gym. A blond man of about forty, with close-cropped hair and sunken cheeks. One afternoon, he had struck up a conversation with me in one of those sorry cafés on the Carrefour de l'Odéon. He was a writer and journalist. I told him that I, too, hoped to become a writer one day. At which point he had given me a condescending smile:

"It's a lot of work, you know . . . A lot of work . . . I don't think you have what it takes . . ."

And he cited the example of a famous young dancer whom he greatly admired, who "worked at the barre day in, day out."

"That's what it means to write, you see . . . Twenty-four hours of exercise a day . . . I doubt you have the strength of character . . . It's not even worth trying."

He had almost persuaded me.

"I can show you how I write . . ."

He invited me to visit him at his place on Rue du Dragon. Two rooms with chalk-white walls, exposed beams in dark wood, a rustic writing table of the same color, and very stiff seats with high backs. He was wearing his sweat suit. He had signed one of his books for me, whose title I've forgotten. To my great surprise, he recommended I read *The Girls* by Montherlant. Then he'd offered to drive me home in his car, a Dauphine Gordini. Over the following months, I had seen him from my window, at night, parked in front of the building in that blue car with white trim. And I was afraid.

I checked to see if by chance it was there today.

But no. Silence. Night had fallen. I preferred the reflections of the streetlamps on the walls to the dim light of the bulb hanging from the ceiling. Once again, I feared Gisèle would never return. The voice I had heard on the phone only heightened my sense of isolation and abandonment. It corresponded so well to this empty office, where I was having trouble remembering where the furniture used to be.

La Petite-Roquette . . . I had been walking one day on the street of the same name and had passed by the prison. Often, in my dreams, Rue de la Roquette spills onto the kind of square you find in Rome, in the middle of which rises a fountain. It's always summer. The square is deserted and flattened by the sun. Nothing disturbs the silence but the murmur of the fountain. And I remain there, in the shadows, waiting for Gisèle to walk out of prison.

The entry door slammed: I recognized her footsteps. She was there, in front of me, in her unbuttoned raincoat. She switched on the light. She said I was making a strange face.

"That man called."

"And?"

I told her it was someone wanting information about my father and that he'd made an appointment to see me later that evening, at ten, in the café just opposite, across the Seine.

"It shouldn't take long."

I took her face in my hands and kissed her. It didn't matter if her name was Gisèle or Suzanne Kraay and if she'd served time in La Petite-Roquette. Had I known her back then, I wouldn't have missed a single opportunity to go visit her. And even if she had committed a crime, I didn't care, so long as she was alive, pressed against me, in her black skirt and pullover.

"Aren't you worried he'll walk in on us?" she whispered in my ear.

At first I thought she meant the man on the telephone. But she was talking about Grabley.

"Oh, no. He's at the Tomate . . ."

Even so, we pushed the couch so that it blocked the office door.

I could see the café lights shining from the other side of the Seine, at the corner of the quay. Was the man already there? I wished I had a very powerful pair of binoculars to watch him with. He, too, from the café, could check whether the lights were on in the apartment windows. And that thought caused me a sudden stab of anxiety, as if a trap had just closed on me.

"What are you looking at?"

She was lying on the couch. Her skirt and pullover were thrown on the coffee table.

"I'm watching for the tour boat," I told her.

I cracked open the window. The Quai de Conti remained empty for a long while, the time it took for the traffic lights to turn green, over toward the Pont-Neuf. And before the next few cars appeared, there was silence, no doubt the same silence my father had known on evenings during the Occupation, behind this same window.

At that time, the café opposite didn't shine and the Louvre Colonnade was shrouded in darkness. The advantage, today, was knowing where the danger lay: that light across the Seine.

I looked at my watch. A quarter to ten.

"I have to go to my appointment."

She was sitting on the edge of the couch. She leaned her chin in the palms of her hands.

"Do you have to go?"

"If I don't, he'll only call back . . . Might as well get rid of him once and for all."

I repeated that he was a former associate of my father's. I was tempted to tell her the truth, but checked myself in time. She wanted to come with me, rather than stay in the apartment by herself. We went out with the dog. She had thought we might walk to the café, crossing via the Pont des Arts. But I said it would be better to take the car.

As we were about to turn onto the Pont du Carrousel, I almost asked her just to keep driving, keep following the river. Then, once on the Right Bank, as we got closer to the café, I thought better of it. I was ready for this meeting now. I was even eager to see this man's face.

We stopped at the corner of Rue du Louvre, in front of the café entrance. Only one customer, sitting near the window. He was reading a newspaper spread out on the table and hadn't noticed our car. I felt Gisèle's hand grip my arm. She was staring at the man, mouth half-open. Her face drained of color.

"Don't go, Jean . . . Please, I'm begging you."

I was struck that she'd called me by my name. She held on to my arm.

"Why? Do you know him?"

He was still reading his paper beneath the fluorescent lights. Before turning a page, he moistened his index finger on his tongue.

"If you go, we're done for . . . I've had dealings with him before . . ."

An expression of terror was twisting her features. But I felt completely calm. I gently caressed her forehead and lips. I felt like kissing her and murmuring comforting words in her ear. I simply said:

"Don't worry about a thing . . . This guy CAN'T HURT US . . ."

She tried again to hold me back, but I opened the door and got out of the car.

"Wait for me here. And if it goes on too long, go back to the apartment."

For the first time in my life, I felt sure of myself. My timidity, my doubts, that habit of apologizing for my every movement, of deprecating myself, of taking the other person's side—all that had vanished, fallen off like dead skin. I was in one of those dreams where you meet the dangers and torments of the present but avoid them at every turn, for you already know the future and feel invulnerable.

I pushed open the glass door. He raised his eyes from his newspaper. A man of about forty, brown hair, bald spot like a monk's tonsure. He was wearing a tan coat.

I planted myself in front of him.

"Mister Guélin, I presume?"

He fixed me with a cold stare, as if gauging how much he was going to make me pay for my apparent nonchalance.

"We'll be better off in back . . ."

His voice was even more metallic than on the phone. Standing in his coat, with his bearing and stocky outline, that baldness over a brutal face, he looked like an ex-soccer player.

We went to sit in back, he on the red imitation-leather bench. There was no one there but us. Except a man in a suit at the counter where they sold cigarettes. But he didn't seem to know we were there.

He sat leaning on the table, elbows spread, still giving me his cold stare, chin slightly raised.

"You did the right thing coming here . . . Otherwise, your situation could have gotten much more difficult . . ."

He tried to make me look away. But he didn't succeed. I had even moved my face closer to his, as if in challenge.

"Something very serious happened yesterday afternoon, in Neuilly . . . You know what I'm talking about?"

"No."

"Really? You're a smart boy and you'd do better to level with me . . ."

I still didn't lower my eyes, and our faces were now so close that our foreheads nearly touched. His breath smelled like anise liqueur.

"First off, you're a minor . . . And your girl-friend has been turning tricks for some time now . . ."

The words had been spoken in a toneless voice, but he was watching for my reaction.

I forced myself to smile at him, a wide smile that must have looked more like a grimace.

"She's a regular at an apartment at 34 Rue Desaix . . . I know the place well, and the madam . . . and even most of the clients . . . As do you, I suppose?"

I remembered the other evening, when I'd waited in front of the buildings. The viaduct of the elevated metro at the end of the street. And the endless wall of the Dupleix barracks. I had seen her come out of one of the buildings and walk toward me.

"I imagine you also know your girlfriend's husband?"

"None of these things are my business."

I had adopted a dreamy, absent tone.

"But of course it's your business. And you are going to tell me in detail what happened yesterday afternoon."

The newspaper was folded in the pocket of his coat. Earlier, I had asked Gisèle to bring me back the same evening paper, but she had forgotten.

"Nothing happened yesterday afternoon."

I had pulled away from him so as not to smell his anise breath. I leaned back against the chair.

"Nothing? You must be joking . . ."

He had folded his arms.

I couldn't take my eyes off the newspaper in his pocket. Perhaps he was going to unfold it and show me the photo of the man we'd seen getting into Ansart's car, tell me they had fished his body out from under the bridge at Puteaux. But the thought of it left me cold. It was only later, around age thirty, that I started feeling some remorse when recalling certain episodes from my past, like a tightrope walker who feels dizzy retrospectively, after he has crossed over the abyss.

"You're coming with me to see some friends. And I advise you to tell us everything, or you'll be in a world of trouble . . ."

His tone brooked no objection and his hard eyes were still fixed on me. I could feel myself losing my footing, so to pluck up my courage, I said:

"Anyway, who are you, exactly?"

"I'm a very close friend of Mister Samson."

What was he trying to insinuate? That he was with the police?

"What does that mean, a very close friend?"

He was taken aback by my question, but then he recovered:

"It means someone who can land you in jail just like that."

And then a strange phenomenon occurred: I still hadn't looked away, and this man was losing his composure. Little by little, he started reminding me of those dozens of individuals who would meet my father in hotel lobbies or cafés just like this one. I often accompanied him. I was fourteen at the time, but I watched all those people under the fluorescent lights. In even the most elegant of them, the ones who at first seemed the most respectable, a cornered street hawker always showed through.

"Because you want to take charge of my schooling?"

The other seemed nonplussed:

"A minute from now, you won't be such a wise guy."

But it was already too late for him. He was receding in time. He would go join all the other bit players, all the poor accessories of a period of my life: Grabley, the woman with straw-blond hair, the Tomate, the unfurnished apartment, an old navy blue overcoat in the crowd of travelers at the Gare de Lyon . . .

"So long, sir."

I was outside. Farther on, on the little square, she had been watching for me. She waved her arm. She had parked the car in the shadow of Saint-Germain-l'Auxerrois church.

"I was afraid he'd take you away with him . . ."

Her hand was trembling. She had to turn the key several times before the ignition caught.

"There was no reason to be afraid," I said.

"He was in the office when the other one interrogated me. But I already knew him from before . . . He didn't say anything about me?"

"No. Nothing."

We followed Rue de Rivoli. Once again, a feeling of euphoria enveloped me. If we continued to roll past these arcades, beyond which streetlights gleamed unto infinity, we would emerge onto a large public square near the seashore. Through the lowered window, I could already smell the ocean air.

"Do you swear he didn't mention me?"

"I swear."

What that phantom had said no longer mattered: La Petite-Roquette, 34 Rue Desaix, and the afternoon in Neuilly when "something very

serious happened." All of it was so far removed
. . . I had made a leap into the future.

"I think it's better if we don't stay at the apartment tonight."

I tried to reassure her that we were in no danger, but she seemed so anxious, so nervous, that I finally said:

"We can go wherever you like."

Still, it gave me a pang in the heart to see her prey to shadows and incidents that to me were already past and done. It was as if I had set sail and was watching her, far behind me, flailing against the tide.

We went back to the Quai de Conti apartment to grab the suitcases. She waited for me at the foot of the small stairway leading to the fifth floor.

Just as I opened the door to the storage closet, the phone rang. She stared at me, petrified.

"Don't answer."

I climbed down the stairs carrying the two

suitcases and walked into the office. The phone was still ringing. I felt for it in the dark:

"Hello."

Silence.

"Are you still in the café, Guélin?" I said.

No reply. I thought I could hear him breathing. She had picked up the listening extension. We were standing near the windows. I couldn't help glancing toward the other bank of the Seine. Over there, the café was lit. I said:

"How's it going, you pathetic old fuck?"

Another breath. It was like the rustle of wind in the leaves. She wanted me to hang up, grabbed the receiver and tried to wrest it from me, but she couldn't. I kept it glued to my ear. One evening, at the same hour, in the same place, during the Occupation, my father had received a similar phone call. No one answered. It was no doubt a man much like the one from before, brown hair, balding, tan coat, who belonged to Superintendent Permilleux's squad and was tasked with ferreting out undeclared Jews.

A crackling sound. He hung up.

"We have to get out of here right now," she said.

She carried one of her suitcases herself, the lighter one, and we crossed the foyer. As we were about to go out, I put down the other suitcase:

"Hold on a moment. I'll be right back . . ."

I ran back up the little staircase. In the fifth-floor bedroom I gathered the few books that still remained on the shelves between the two windows, among which I found *To the Happy Few*.

I piled them on the bed and knotted one of the sheets into a bundle. Those books had been shelved there well before my father's arrival in the apartment. It was the previous tenant, the author of *The Hunt*, who had left them. Some of them bore the name, on the flyleaf, of a mysterious François Vernet.

When I came back down with my improvised bag, she was waiting on the landing.

I slammed the door shut and felt as if I were leaving that apartment forever, because of the books I was taking with me.

*   *   *

This time we had left the dog in the car. Seeing us, he let out a kind of howl and danced up and down on his hind legs.

We stashed the two suitcases and the bundle of books in the trunk.

"Where to?" I asked.

"To that hotel where I'd taken a room."

I thought of the night porter, his lantern jaw and thin lips, the disdainful look he'd given us the other night. But now, I wasn't even afraid of him anymore.

Nor was she, because she said:

"We should have given him some money and he would have looked the other way."

I turned to her.

"Do you have enough money to go to Rome?"

"Yes. I've saved up thirty thousand francs."

With the money from Dell'Aversano and the amount from Ansart, that made more than forty thousand between us.

"I've put half of it in one of the suitcases and I hid the rest in the house in Saint-Leu-la-Forêt. I'll have to go get it tomorrow."

I didn't dare ask her where that money came from. Was it her husband's savings? Or what she had earned at 34 Rue Desaix, in that apartment the man had mentioned earlier? But none of that was important. It was past. In Rome, one spring evening, we would start living our real lives. We would have forgotten all those years of adolescence, and even the names of our parents.

We drove along the quays. The dark façade of the Gare d'Orsay, with its rusted awnings that no longer opened onto anything. And the hotel, in the same building as the station. We stopped at a red light, and I peered in at the entrance and reception desk.

She said:

"You want to take a room here?"

We would have been the only customers in that hotel, which from outside was indistinguishable from the decommissioned train station.

Sometimes I dream that I'm with her, in the middle of the reception lobby. The night porter is wearing a threadbare stationmaster's uniform. He comes over to hand us our key. The elevator no longer works and we climb up a marble stairway. On the first floor, we try in vain to find our room. We pass through the large dining room shrouded in darkness and get lost in the corridors. We end up in an old waiting room lit by a single naked bulb in the ceiling. We sit on the only surviving bench. The station is no longer operational, but you never know: the train for Rome might pass through, by mistake, and stop for a few seconds, just long enough for us to climb aboard.

We parked the car at the corner of Avenue de Suffren and the small street where the hotel was. I carried the two suitcases, and she the bundle of books. The dog walked in front of us, off his leash.

The hotel door wasn't closed like the first time. The same night porter was standing behind the reception desk. He didn't recognize us right off. He cast a suspicious eye on the bundled bedsheet Gisèle was carrying and on the dog.

"We'd like a room," said Gisèle.

"We don't rent rooms for just one night," said the porter in glacial tones.

"Well, then, for two weeks," I said in a gentle voice. "And I'll pay you in cash, if you prefer."

I pulled from the pocket of my coat the wad of bills that Dell'Aversano had given me.

He looked interested. He said:

"I'll have to charge half-price extra for the dog."

It was at that moment that he recognized me. He fixed his croupier's eye on me.

"You were here the other night . . . You were the young lady's brother . . . Except, you still have to prove it . . ."

I slid a few hundred-franc bills into the breast pocket of his jacket. His gaze softened.

"Thank you, sir."

He turned around and pulled a key from one of the cubbyholes.

"Room number 3 for you and your sister . . ."

He was now extending us every professional courtesy.

"It's on the first floor."

He handed me the key and leaned forward.

"Make no mistake . . . The hotel now only

occupies the first floor of the building. The rest are furnished apartments."

He smiled.

"Obviously, it's not strictly by the book . . . But neither are many things in life, am I right?"

I had taken the key, a simple tin key that didn't look like it fit a hotel room.

"For the bill, I'm afraid I can't give you a receipt."

He looked truly apologetic.

"Don't give it another thought," I said. "It's much better this way."

We climbed the stairs, which were covered with a worn red carpet.

Several doors on either side of the hallway. Each one bore a number written in pencil.

We went into room number 3. It was spacious and high-ceilinged. A bay window looked out on the street. The very wide bed had baby blue sheets and a plaid blanket. A small wooden staircase led up to a mezzanine. The dog lay down on the floor at the foot of the bed.

"We could stay here until we leave for Rome," said Gisèle.

Of course. While waiting for that day, we would not leave the neighborhood, just like airline passengers at the departure gate before boarding. We wouldn't even leave this room, or this bed. And I imagined the man in the tan coat from before, ringing at the door of the Quai de Conti apartment early in the morning, coming for us as he had done twenty years earlier for my father and as he would do for all eternity. But he would never get his hands on us.

"What are you thinking about?" she asked.

"Rome."

She switched off the bedside lamp. We were on the bed and we hadn't drawn the curtains over the large bay window. I heard voices and slamming car doors from the garage across the way. The light from its electric sign fell on us. Soon all became quiet. I feel her lips on my temple and in the hollow of my ear. She asks, in a whisper, if I love her.

The next day, we got up at around ten. There was no one at the reception desk. We had breakfast on Rue du Laos, in a café with the same name as the street.

She said she was going straight out to retrieve the rest of the money in Saint-Leu-la-Forêt and hoped "it would go well." Yes, she risked running into her husband and other people who lived in the house. But in the end, what difference did it make? She no longer owed anything to anyone.

I offered to go with her, but she maintained it was best if she went alone.

"I'll call you in an hour if I need you."

We went back to the hotel so that she could jot down the number. The porter still wasn't there but on the counter we found a pile of buff-colored cards on which was written: "Hôtel-pension Ségur—furnished apartments, 7-bis Rue de la Cavalerie (15th), SUFFREN 75-55." She slipped one into the pocket of her raincoat.

We walked to the car. She held my arm. She wanted to take the dog with her. She sat at the wheel and he on the back seat. I found a pretext not to leave her quite yet. Could she drop me at a newsstand?

She followed Avenue de Suffren toward the Seine. She stopped at the first newsstand.

"See you in a bit."

She leaned out of the lowered window and waved.

I shoved the newspaper in my pocket. I turned onto the first street I came to, on the left, followed it, and emerged onto a square in the middle of which stretched a large public green with a gazebo.

I sat on one of the benches near the gazebo to read the paper. In front of me was the façade of the Dupleix barracks.

Sun. A cloudless sky. On the bench next to mine, a brown-haired woman of about thirty was watching a little boy ride his bike.

I was surprised to hear the clack of horse-shoes coming nearer. A group of horsemen in military dress were riding into the barracks. I remembered that on Sunday mornings in my childhood, I used to hear the same sound when the Republican Guard paraded by on the quay.

On the local news page, I didn't find the picture of the man they'd made get in their car on Sunday afternoon. Nothing about Ansart or Jacques de Bavière, or about Martine Gaul.

It occurred to me that we'd been right near here the other evening and I decided to walk to Rue Desaix, without having a clear idea of where it was. But I had only to skirt the barracks wall.

I recognized the building at number 34. Yes, that was where I had waited for her. The viaduct of the elevated metro, to the left, blocked the horizon of the street. What floor was the apartment on?

I took the same path and, once again, I came out onto the square with the public green, in front of the barracks.

I rejoined Avenue de Suffren and the narrow street with our hotel.

There was still nobody at the reception desk. The phone was sitting on the wooden ledge beneath the cubbyholes. It was nearly one o'clock. I leaned my elbow on the desk. One o'clock. One-fifteen. The phone didn't ring. I picked up the receiver to make sure it was working properly and heard the dial tone.

She had arranged to meet me at two, at the café on Rue du Laos. I had no desire to go back up to our room. I went out and took Avenue de Suffren, but this time in the other direction. The avenue was quieter on this side. Along the opposite sidewalk, the old buildings of the Ecole Militaire. And the rows of plane trees. We wouldn't see their leaves next spring because we would be in Rome.

The more I walked, the more it felt as if I was in a foreign city and becoming someone else. What I had lived through in my childhood and the few years following, up to my meeting Gisèle, gently peeled off of me in strips, dissolved; now and then, I even made a small effort to retain a few scraps before they vanished into thin air: the years of boarding school, my father's silhouette in his navy blue coat, my mother, Grabley, the lights of the tour boat on the bedroom ceiling . . .

At ten minutes to two, I was standing in front of the café on Rue du Laos. She wasn't there yet. I wanted to buy her a bouquet of roses at the florist's, but I didn't have any money on me. I walked back to the hotel. When I went in, the night porter was standing behind the reception desk.

He stared at me and blushed violently.

"Sir . . ."

He couldn't find the words, but I had understood even before hearing them. Your friend. Accident. Just after the Suresnes bridge. They had found the hotel card in her raincoat pocket and called here.

I walked out, my mind a blank. Outside, everything was light, clear, indifferent, like a pure blue January sky.

PATRICK MODIANO, winner of the 2014 Nobel Prize in Literature, was born in Boulogne-Billancourt, France, in 1945, and was educated in Annecy and Paris. He published his first novel, *La Place de l'Etoile,* in 1968. In 1978, he was awarded the Prix Goncourt for *Rue des Boutiques Obscures* (published in English as *Missing Person*), and in 1996 he received the Grand Prix National des Lettres for his body of work. Modiano's other writings include a book-length interview with the writer Emmanuel Berl and, with Louis Malle, the screenplay for *Lacombe Lucien.*

MARK POLIZZOTTI's books include the collaborative novel *S.* (1991), *Lautréamont Nomad* (1994), *Revolution of the Mind: The Life of André Breton* (Farrar, Straus and Giroux, 1995; rev. ed., 2009), *Luis Buñuel's Los Olvidados* (British Film Institute, 2006), and *Bob Dylan: Highway 61 Revisited* (Continuum, 2006). His articles and reviews have appeared in the *New Republic,* the *Wall Street Journal, ARTnews,* the *Nation, Parnassus, Partisan Review, Bookforum,* and elsewhere. The translator of more than forty books from the French, including works by Gustave Flaubert, Marguerite Duras, André Breton, Raymond Roussel, and Jean Echenoz, as well as other works by Patrick Modiano, he directs the publications program at The Metropolitan Museum of Art in New York.

Explore the Margellos World Republic of Letters—great works of literature, available in English for the first time.

Also by Patrick Modiano

Paris Nocturne

Pedigree

Suspended Sentences

The Dirty Dust
Cré na Cille
Máirtín Ó Cadhain

The Last Lover
Can Xue

Five Spice Street
Can Xue

The Roar of Morning
Tip Marugg

Masters and Servants
Pierre Michon

Origin of the World
Pierre Michon

Rimbaud the Son
Pierre Michon

Winter Mythologies
and Abbots
Pierre Michon